FIRST B...

T5-AXS-387

LOVE'S PERFECT IMAGE

Judy Baer

Serenade/Serenata
BOOKS
of the Zondervan Publishing House
Grand Rapids, Michigan

Love's Perfect Image
Copyright © 1984 by The Zondervan Corporation
1415 Lake Drive, S.E.
Grand Rapids, MI 49506

ISBN 0-310-46522-2

Edited by Anne Severance and Nancye Willis
Designed by Kim Koning

Printed in the United States of America

85   86   87   88   89 / 10   9   8   7   6   5   4   3   2

To Adrienne and Jennifer—
may you grow to be lovely
inside and out.

CHAPTER ONE

THE LOCKER ROOM DOOR swung shut, revealing a tall, lovely girl in the three-way mirror behind it. Jayne Lindstrom, as usual, was surprised to realize it was her own reflection she had so fleetingly admired. Still unfamiliar with the lithe, trim body she had molded here at Body Images Health Club, she expected to see the sad-eyed, plump, matronly figure she had so recently shed.

Still unaccustomed to the willowy legs and trim torso in mauve tights and fuchsia leotard, she admired the image as she would a unique carving in the gallery window next door, then turned away, afraid that when she looked back the vision would be gone, and the thick hips and unsightly midriff of her former detested Rubenesque figure would be in its place.

Unaccustomed to pride in her physical appearance, Jayne fretted a little, allowing a troubled frown to slip across her even features and reached for a teal blue smock with the words *Body Images* emblazoned across the bodice. She was far more comfortable hiding herself in its generous folds. Steam rose then from the shower room, frosting the mirror with a glaze of opaque fog, obscuring the dark-haired vision.

Hurrying from the steamy pink-and-silver locker room into the briskly cool hallway, Jayne felt the jolt of sudden temperature change just before she ran with a resounding thump, face-to-face and chest-to-chest into her business partner. Chad Richards appeared to be traveling in an equal hurry in the opposite direction.

Her breath left her, not due to the jolt, but because of her proximity to the man, so close that his cologne, sweet and spicy, wafted into her nostrils and she could feel his warm breath on her cheek. She normally kept her distance from Chad. Theirs was a good working relationship and she was unwilling to jeopardize it by allowing her attraction to him to become apparent.

He is gorgeous, she admitted to herself as her eyes slid over Chad's deeply tanned and muscled calves and thighs. His white shorts showed off his well-formed legs to their best advantage.

"Whoa! You'll wipe out a client someday shooting out from behind closed doors like that!" Waving aside her attempts at apology, Chad continued in his agreeable, bantering tone, "Actually, it was one of the nicest encounters I've had today. Maybe we could work it into the program somewhere: 'Maintain good mental health—bump into a beautiful girl each day!'"

Unable to restrain a smile, Jayne laid a slim,

manicured hand on the sleeve of Chad's sweat-shirt-clad arm. She could feel the hard, sinewy flexor muscle beneath.

"Your charm never wavers, does it, Chad? I've interrupted your hasty exit and you're still the gentleman. You were supposed to be out of here three hours ago. Now scram before it's time to check in again!"

Admiring the even expanse of ivory teeth and lightly clefted chin, Jayne wondered how Chad managed to stay so pleasant and unruffled, even after a twelve-hour day. Perhaps Chad Richards was one of the lucky ones—no past to haunt him, no fears to wrestle. . . .

"Look who's talking!" Chad's voice, deep and melodious, broke into her reverie. "Buddy said he'd close up tonight, and the last of the racquet-ball players are through. Everybody is showering. Fifteen minutes, and we're free agents. How about coming out for a cup of coffee with me, Jayne?" He entwined his fingers in the mane of hair flooding down her back and tugged gently.

Her heart began to thud in an unaccustomed way. She pulled away, wary of his touch. Not many men as attractive as Chad paid her such flamboyant attention.

Tingles of surprise played up and down her spine. A man like Chad Richards did not have other plans for a summer Saturday night? Perpetually tanned, with sun-streaked blond hair, Chad was the focus of admiration for 99 percent of the women who belonged to the club. Just at this moment, the errant forelock which persisted in

7

dropping over sea-green eyes was acting up again, and he combed it back with fingers widespread. Jayne almost melted.

Suspecting that his invitation was only a polite gesture, however, she flashed a regretful smile. "Thanks, but no thanks, Chad. Not tonight. Maybe another time." Inwardly chastising herself for her tormenting insecurity, she resigned herself to another evening alone.

"You've said *that* before!" he protested. "A million times, maybe more, over the last eight months! I'm getting a little tired of rejection. Are you trying to give me an inferiority complex?"

Startled by the ludicrous suggestion, Jayne laughed aloud. "You should attend to the one of a hundred women who are absolutely cow-eyed over you, Chad Richards. To me you are the perfect business partner, racquetball player extraordinaire, and all-time, top-notch flirt!"

"So that's it! You don't believe I'm serious! Well, I am and I'll *prove* it." Suddenly earnest, he took Jayne's slim, pale hands into his own long tanned ones and looked from his impressive height down into her startled brown eyes. His facial expression changed and the bantering look was gone. A warm light gleamed in his eyes.

"Don't come with me tonight, Jayne—come tomorrow, instead. I'd like you to go to church with me at nine-thirty, then to the finest place in town for Sunday brunch. They serve everything from eggs Benedict to smoked salmon. It's the best possible way to spend a day off—food for the soul and then some for the body. You look frazzled. I think you need both."

8

It had always amazed Jayne to think of Chad in church. He seemed such an unlikely candidate. Sunday morning yachting seemed more his style, yet he made no bones about his faith. Jayne had placed so little emphasis on things spiritual in her early years that someone who professed a faith and lived it was a novelty to her, a new and unique species to be watched with suspicion—and grudging admiration.

Jayne had only a faint recollection, almost a dream, of going to church with her grandmother as a young girl. Later, when she felt pulled in that direction, Ed, her one and only boyfriend during those frustrating years, had scoffed at her curiosity. Afraid of losing the one man who had shown an interest in her, Jayne had abandoned her better judgment and allowed Ed Garrett to monopolize the hours of her days.

What good had it done? Jayne mused to herself, suddenly miles away from the impatient tapping of Chad's foot as he waited for an answer. Ed had left her anyway—on the arm of a woman half Jayne's size and had never looked back to see the pain and hurt of rejection in her wide umber eyes.

"Well, *will* you?" Chad's persistence was touching. "Listen, they serve every fresh fruit known to man and invent new ones on a regular basis! A croissant and fruit will not put an ounce on that gorgeous frame. Come *on*, Jayne!"

Something washed over her then—a desire to enjoy a day in the company of a fascinating man. She was no longer the plain, sad girl of her childhood, but a mature woman, free to make her own choices.

"Wheedling is not necessary, Chad." She adopted a pseudodignified pose and lifted her short, straight nose into the air in a comic attempt at patrician dignity. "You discovered my Achilles' heel. If I can eat and be guaranteed of not falling off this perpetual diet of mine, I'll go with you." Patting the flat expanse of stomach under her smock, Jayne accepted Chad's appealing invitation.

Amazed at her acquiescence, Jayne wondered at the man who could make her break her self-imposed hibernation from the social world.

Chad, however, was still not satisfied.

"And *church*, Jayne. That's the most important part."

Bantering at a halt, his voice lowered to a reverent tone. His eyes took on the emerald of a field after a spring shower, clear and sparkling.

Suddenly unsure of her decision, Jayne hesitated. "I don't know, Chad. It's been such a long time . . . I just don't think I'd be comfortable. Maybe I'd better pass after all. Anyway," she said, forcing a brighter tone to her voice, "I'd planned to come in tomorrow morning and finish up the books. I've got new membership cards to mail out, and bills to pay . . ."

"On *Sunday morning?*" Incredulity rang in Chad's voice. "We're closed then for a reason, Jayne. It's our day of rest!"

"Yours maybe, not mine," she rejoined, irritated by his light criticism. "Why do you think the desk runs so smoothly on Monday mornings?

10

Because I've been catching up and organizing when it's not so wild in here—that's why!"

Jayne could see the lovely brunch, the moments with Chad, slipping away. They could never seem to agree on this. Chad was adamant about his day off and what he did with it. He'd even mentioned once a Bible study group that met on Sunday evenings. Jayne, on the other hand, worked furiously on the lesson plans for her classes, ate a light supper, and spent the remainder of the evening mindlessly in front of her television set.

"We'll never get together on this, Chad. Thanks for the invitation, but maybe it would be best if I just stayed home."

Emitting a theatrical sigh of disappointment, Chad began tugging his fingers back through his sun-streaked hair in apparent but controlled frustration. "Jayne, what am I going to do with you? We've been partners for eight months, and I can't even pull you away for one morning—just to get to know you a little better!"

Their relationship had been an odd one, Jayne had to admit, the common denominator being Buddy Carlisle, their third partner. Buddy, a weightlifter and teddy bear of a man, had watched Jayne's metamorphosis from dowdy to chic, heavy to slender, and had suggested that she buy into the business and help him create a truly all-encompassing health club facility. A few weeks later, enter third partner, Chad Richards, and the predicament she found herself in today.

"I'm just not accustomed to handsome men wanting to take me out, Chad. And especially not

11

to church. It all still scares me witless. Someday I'll explain, but for now I think I'll just go home. Thanks, anyway.''

Laying her smooth cheek against his in an unaffected embrace, she squeezed his broad shoulders and then walked off, the Body Images smock billowing out behind her. His fragrance, so tangy and masculine, filled her nostrils and sent her pulse racing as rapidly as the most strenuous workout.

Chad stood at the end of the hall watching her departure, his legs spread wide and braced stiffly, arms crossed so tightly that the biceps bulged under his shirt, a puzzled expression on his bronzed face and something akin to hurt and disappointment in his sea-green eyes. Those eyes followed her down the long corridor until the door swung shut behind her and she vanished into the night.

Outside, Jayne took a gulp of fresh air, struggling to rid herself of the huge lump in her throat. Leaning against the building until the shaking subsided in her legs, she walked to her car, mind racing.

Chad Richards as a business partner was more than she had bargained for. His degree in business administration was only the tip of the iceberg where his talents were concerned. He was a magnificent teacher, his every class—from racquetball and tennis to handball and squash— was filled as soon as the schedules were posted. But his charm was intimidating. Relatively inexperienced with men, Jayne was terrified of a man who could have any beautiful girl he wanted.

Suspicious, she wondered what his ulterior motive might be.

"Why me?" The question slipped out, startling her with its sound on the quiet night air. "Why me?" she asked again, more loudly. Visions of a fat girl in matronly clothing and unstyled hair assaulted her memory. That was Jayne Lindstrom—plain, insecure, vulnerable. Only in those moments when she did not recognize herself in a mirror or store window did she realize that the new Jayne Lindstrom was something more—a slim, lovely and successful businesswoman—more than Ed Garrett had ever thought she could be.

Ed Garrett. His face came easily to mind. A dark and appealing young man, Jayne could still envision his blue-violet eyes and wide, sensuous mouth.

Oh, what a fool I made of myself over him! Standing in a pitch-dark parking lot, three hundred miles from the childhood home of the *old* Jayne Lindstrom, the plump, insecurity-fraught girl Ed Garrett had idly wooed, she blushed even now, almost ten years later.

Slipping into her sports car, she turned the ignition, flipped on the stereo and slid back the sun roof. She wanted the wind to whip from her mind the thoughts of the evening, and blank out the painful memories from the past that were churning within her.

The car responded to her slightest touch, dispelling her stormy thoughts with its fine-tuned response. This was her symbol of success, this silver machine at her command. Body Images had allowed her this triumph over the expectations of family and friends. Taunted as a child for her size, her pudding bowl haircut and worn hand-me-downs, this car and the sleek new body she had fashioned were the symbols of victorious conquest over the past. Sadly, the scars of painful gibes and taunting laughter still remained. Pulling into her parking space in the garage under the condominium, Jayne locked up and headed for the elevator.

Trendy and ultrachic, the building typified the people who lived here. The residence of several ambitious, young business executives, successful models, and wealthy surgeons, HighTower Court was an elite and expensive hideaway. High-quality, original artwork decorated the halls, and plush, velvety carpets muffled the random footsteps. Jayne considered an apartment at HighTower another feather in her cap, a consolation prize for the years dedicated to her career as chief dietician at University Hospital—years when her friends were marrying and having children.

She did find it odd, though, how everything related to food had always been her source of both pain and comfort. Shrugging her shoulders, she unlocked her door and stepped inside.

Relieved to be home where she could let down her guard, Jayne traveled around the cool, ivory room, letting her fingers touch and slide over the *objets d'art*, strategically placed. Chrome and crystal, wood and glass, textures of every sort greeted her. Wool weavings, white on white, graced the walls. Bunches of wild grasses and wheat filled baskets and pottery vases.

The tension eased as she prepared for bed, savoring the silkiness of her gown and the fresh, clean smell of the sheets. Soon only the gnawing remembrance of Chad's hurt look remained to haunt her along with his appeal: "And *church*, Jayne. That's the most important part!"

CHAPTER TWO

SUNLIGHT FILTERED THROUGH the mint-colored batiste drapes at Jayne's bedroom window, and a soft breeze ruffled them lazily. Jayne stretched and yawned like a contented kitten on the matching minty green sheets of the king-size bed. Propping herself up on her elbows, she was reminded once again how much she loved this room with its monochromatic hues.

"It's like waking in a fresh green pasture, bathed in sunlight," the decorator had said, and Jayne had to agree, relishing the pastoral setting. Burrowing deep into the bedclothes for a few more minutes of sleep, Jayne nearly failed to hear the persistent *tink-tink-tink* of her doorbell.

Jumping up and hastily gathering a hand-quilted robe about herself, she pattered to the screen by her door and pushed the visual button. Before her, standing in the lobby foyer, appeared Chad, dressed in a dark, slim-cut suit and a shirt so painfully white it gleamed even across the building's security system. In his hands was a bouquet of flowers, wrapped carelessly in green florist's paper and tumbling in a riot of color. He was tapping his foot with impatience.

Surprised, amused, and inordinately pleased, Jayne pushed the admittance button and Chad dove for the door and disappeared from sight. Knowing he would be on her doorstep in a matter of seconds, she tugged on the robe, drew the comb from the pocket, and pulled her dark mane of hair into some semblance of order. As she slid the comb back into her pocket, Chad's fisted hand pummelled the door.

Throwing it open, she invited him in with a sweep of her arm and a look of mock dismay on her face.

Not allowing her time to protest, Chad began his patter. "Good morning, fair lady! Undaunted by your rejection of last evening, I decided to take the initiative and pick you up anyway. Don't say anything." He held up a hand in warning. "You have nearly an hour to get ready, and I have a table reserved for brunch later. Give it a try, okay?"

Suddenly his confidence did not seem overbearing, and his plea was so sincere that Jayne weakened for reasons she did not fully understand. "Oh, all right. Just this *once*. But, remember, this is not my style."

"Okay, okay. Just see how you feel about it, Jayne. I think you're missing something big in your life and just don't realize it."

Looking obliquely at him, Jayne thought to

herself, *I am, Chad, but it's self-confidence, not religion that I've been missing.*

Conceding temporary defeat, she splayed her fingers in front of his face.

"Give me ten minutes to dress and ten more to put on my face." She turned and headed toward her room.

"Leave on the old face for me. I like it a lot!" Chad called after her, already making himself at home with the Sunday paper on the expanse of ivory sectional sofa that filled the room. The flowers were scattered around him in lovely disarray.

Jayne turned and grinned. She found herself unaccountably warmed by the sight of the handsome man at home in her private haven. His careless compliment was like a badge of approval, and the insecure Jayne Lindstrom needed all the approval she could get.

Exactly twenty minutes later, Chad gave a long, low whistle as Jayne made her entrance. In place of the cozy robe was a sleek white silk dress, accented only by a wide black cummerbund that encircled her tiny waist in a tight band. Black slides encased her feet with a narrow leather upper, more decorative than functional. Over her dark chestnut hair she wore a large, saucer-like hat, pulled low, revealing nothing until she tipped her head slightly upward and disclosed the merry twinkle in her eyes.

"Look who just stepped out of the pages of *Fashion Today*! Jayne, you're lovelier than ever. You've got to stop schlumping around in that tent of a smock you wear at work. You're the best advertisement we've got!"

"I'm not exactly an exhibitionist, Chad. It's only in the last year that I've been this slim, you know. I spent nearly twenty-nine years in a fat body, and the mental image that goes with obesity doesn't disappear overnight."

She noticed a tiny frown flicker across Chad's features, but it was gone before she was even sure it had been there, and his words belied any problem.

"Exhibitionism is hardly the word for it! I have women every day stopping by the main desk to tell me what a tremendous job you're doing with the aerobic classes and nutrition seminars. Don't tell me numbers don't count! I'm the business administrator and I know that every one of your classes is filled for the next four months!"

"Aha! You love me for my earning potential. I knew there was a reason you were so nice to me." Pointing an accusing finger his way, she wagged it saucily, refusing to be caught up in a serious discussion.

"*Agggggggh!*" Roaring in mock frustration, Chad pulled at his hair. "How can a person get to know the real Jayne Lindstrom! Those protective walls of yours are pretty nearly invincible."

Eyes warm and penitent under the big hat, Jayne touched one pink-tipped nail to Chad's clean-shaven cheek. "I let those walls down once, and the enemy got in and hurt me. I can't let it happen again. Fat girls are more vulnerable than thin ones, Chad. I'm still just a fat girl in a thin body."

19

"But I'm not the enemy, Jayne. Remember that." His voice was so low she could barely hear it, and there seemed to be genuine sorrow for the sensitive woman who had been so deeply hurt.

"I don't know who made you feel this way, Jayne, but I'd like to be the one who helps the wounds heal."

She did not even comprehend his last words, for the face of the young Ed Garrett wheeled in her mind, his last cruel words taunting her, "You're a nice girl, Jayne, but there's just too much of you. . . ."

All her hopes for the future had ended on those words and a new existence had begun for the sole purpose of revenge. Jayne Lindstrom had vowed then to become slim, beautiful, desirable—and unattainable. She dreamed that one day Ed Garrett would regret ever letting her get away.

Tapping her toe on the thick carpet in a gesture borrowed from Chad, she purposefully altered the mood of the moment, "Did you ask me out for brunch or didn't you?" And before Chad could get the words out of his already open mouth, she added, "And *church*, too! Well, let's go!"

Grinning broadly and taking her gently by the arm, they left the room, but not before Chad poked the stem of a stray flower through the black band of her hat, adding a splash of red to the vision in black and white.

Organ music drifted through the open doors of the picturesque chapel. Gray-white stone grouted

with a gray mortar formed the rectangular structure, giving a base for its towering steeple. Set
back from the street, with a cobblestone walk
winding through a thick, carpet-like lawn, the
scene was a panoramic picture of a quiet country
church. Ivy had grown rampant over one side of
the building and was curling its way up the roof.
Rosebushes planted along the perimeter were in
glorious bloom, their reds and greens playing
against the structure in a post card perfect scene.

"Why, this is absolutely lovely, Chad! How
did you discover this place? It's so peaceful!"

"I've been coming here ever since I moved to
Minneapolis from Wisconsin. It reminded me of
the building where I worshipped as a child. My
family comments on it every time they come to
visit. The people are fine and warm and the
fellowship is terrific. You'll have to come to
Bible study and . . ."

"Hold it! I said I'd come to church *once—not
every time the doors are open!*"

Resolute, Jayne dashed Chad's hopes, forcing
him to remember that her interests lay else-
where.

Undaunted, Chad smiled his most charming
smile and steered her into the sanctuary.

The hour passed. Jayne's discomfort subsided
as the music swelled around her and the comforting words flowed. Not really listening to the
spoken word but rather to her senses, Jayne felt
the oneness and joy of this group, so unlike
anything she had ever experienced before. Comforting words like *forgiveness, peace,* and *joy*
drifted into her consciousness as the white-robed

pastor spoke. Yet those words prodded at a need in her. She struggled against them, looking around the room.

Observing Chad out of the corner of her eye, she was amazed by the intent expression on his face. He really loved this! With his head bent in prayer, eyes closed, he was as handsome a man as she had ever seen, his perfectly chiseled profile reflecting some inner peace she could not fathom.

When the bright recessional rang out, people tumbled joyously into the aisles, shaking hands and greeting one another warmly. Suddenly aware of a familiar feeling of not belonging, Jayne edged as quickly as she could toward the exit, but not before Chad grabbed her arm and steered her toward a white-haired, smiling woman at the doorway.

"This is Bessie Norheim, another good Scandinavian like yourself. Bessie, meet Jayne Lindstrom." Chad beamed on the older woman like he'd just discovered a rare and precious treasure.

As Jayne extended a cool hand, she found herself wrapped in an embrace, warm and full of love.

"Welcome to our church, Jayne. Please come back again. Chad, do bring her! I want to get to know her better." Never before had Jayne seen such genuine affection in a person's eyes, nor had she ever been welcomed so unreservedly. Stunned and charmed, she stammered out a thank-you and slipped through the door with Chad close on her heels.

"Isn't Bessie something? She's our number-one welcoming committee. As a matter of fact, she's part of the reason I joined this church. Anyone with that much Christian love just has to share it.''

Ill at ease with the direction of the conversation, Jayne attempted to draw Chad from his favorite topic into an area in which she felt more comfortable.

''Where's the restaurant, Chad? My stomach is getting louder than that pipe organ!''

''Three blocks from here. Look for the place with the doorman and striped awnings over the door. First-class all the way!''

With that they strolled down the street hand-in-hand. Jayne did not even notice until they were nearly at their destination.

Inside, the maitre d' led them to a table near the wall, secluded, yet only steps away from a sumptuous buffet table laden with meats, pastries, fruits, and cheeses. A smaller table to the left held trays of steaming foods—eggs Benedict; waffles; French toast; mounds of sausage, bacon, and ham. The table to the right displayed petits fours, balls of ice cream rolled in coconut and drenched in fudge sauce, kept cool in long trays of crushed ice, and delectable sweets Jayne couldn't begin to name. The centerpiece was a huge, fileted smoked salmon, the pink meat glistening in the light of the crystal chandeliers. Tiny, glittering black and red beads of caviar surrounded it.

Jayne gazed at the feast in amazement, unaware that her mouth had fallen open until Chad shut it gently with a steady finger placed under her chin.

Giggling, Jayne turned to him. "You really meant it when you said this was the best place in town for brunch, didn't you?"

"Absolutely. Would I lie to you? Now are you ready to begin?" Pretending to lick his chops in gluttonous glee, he headed for the groaning tables.

An hour later, sated and relaxed, they sipped their coffee and chatted idly. Chad folded a petit four paper into a tiny ball as he spoke, fingers betraying his nervousness.

"Jayne, something has come up that I believe we need to think about."

"I'm too full to think, Chad. Breathing is even a problem!" She leaned back in her chair and began tugging at the cummerbund.

Reaching for her hands across the table, he took them into his own, caressing them gently, kneading each finger with a firm and steady pressure.

"Today has taught me that this is a relationship I'd like to pursue. You're charming, intelligent, and wonderful to be with." Chad's fingers tightened imperceptibly around hers at the sight of fear flickering in her eyes. "Don't keep me at a distance, Jayne. I won't hurt you!" She struggled to escape his grip, but he would not release her hands.

A surge of the old insecurity flooded her brain. What kind of game was Chad playing? He could have any woman he wanted. Couldn't he *see* that

Jayne Lindstrom could never compete with his own physical attractiveness? If she began to care for him, or more accurately, let him know how much she already cared, he could hurt her. She knew in her heart that she could not bear to be wounded like that again.

Sitting sharply erect, she retorted, the ice in her voice not reflecting the flame in her heart, "Chad, we must remember that we are business partners *first*, acquaintances second. It's a mistake to become romantically involved. Besides, I've been unwise in love before. I can't afford to make the same mistake again."

With tears glistening on her cheeks, Jayne rose and fled, leaving Chad, tapping his foot furiously against the parquet floor.

CHAPTER THREE

WRETCHED AND DISTRAUGHT, Jayne hailed the first taxi and returned to her condominium. Strains of the old childhood taunt rang in her ears: "Plain Jayne, Plain Jayne, won't fit on a train!"

How could I have let this happen? she thought. Somewhere there was a chink in her armor. Her defenses down, Chad had slipped into her life and heart, opening her up for more heartache.

In her haste to gain the protection of her living room, Jayne almost missed the note taped to her mailbox. But it rustled in the breeze as the door opened, and she grabbed it with her free hand, crumpling it slightly as she made her way toward the apartment.

Once inside, she kicked off the wispy shoes, and flung the hat like a frisbee across the room, where it landed, shuddering, on a contemporary wooden sculpture. Spreading the note out on the glass and chrome coffee table, she smoothed away the wrinkles and began to read.

Jayne—
I'm in Minneapolis on business and thought for kicks I'd look you up. Call you tonight.

Ed

The floor and ceiling seemed to change places and the room whirled around her, carousel fashion, as she sank to the ivory sectional. *So Ed has come back.* It was the thing she had dreamed of all those torturous months of self-denial. This was what kept her for hours in the exercise room at the club—bending, stretching, writhing—until her body responded to every mental command and was toned and sleek. She held her nutrition students in awe with her rigid regimen and the glowing hair and skin that had resulted.

All of that was gone for the moment, and the former Jayne Lindstrom was back, vulnerable and defenseless against the past she perceived so painfully.

I wish Chad were here. The thought surprised and comforted her. Chad had so much faith in her, in himself, in his God. Remembering his presence beside her in church, his admiring gaze and the love that his friend Bessie showered on her was consoling.

I am not a bad and worthless being! The thought came to her, unbidden. Unaccustomed to such a positive notion, Jayne took heart in it anyway, smiling slightly. Chad's positive outlook was having some influence. She had achieved what she had set out to do. She was a successful businesswoman, appealing, at least, to Chad. The weight was gone, as were the unattractive clothes.

If Chad sees something in me, perhaps now Ed will, too. Conceivably, this unaccustomed, new-found beauty was the tool she needed. Her time for revenge had come. Ed Garrett would see what he had missed . . . and regret his mistake!

Bouyed by the prospects, Jayne stood. There was a lot to be done before Ed called . . . .

At 7:00 P.M. Jayne heard the doorbell. Instinctively she knew Ed had decided to appear on her doorstep rather than call. And a quick glance in the mirror confirmed that she was ready for him.

Her slim figure was encased in a sleek aquamarine silk dress that followed every bend and curve. Fine gold chains were layered across the expanse of her ivory neck, and glinted in the dimmed light like so many tiny stars. Hammered gold globes winked at her ear lobes, and diamonds glittered in the dinner ring on her ruby-tipped finger. Her dark hair, full and lush, flowed down her back in a fragrant cascade—a single aquamarine silk flower nestled in its depths. Wisps of golden straps slippered her slender feet.

Looking about her, Jayne was pleased with the atmosphere she had created. Candlelight softened the harsh edges of the room, bathing everything in mellow hues. The music of Tchaikovsky filled the room, lilting from hidden speakers. The fragrance of fresh-cut flowers permeated the air with a delicate perfume.

The bell persisted. The jarring note signaled another presence, disturbing and forceful. Taking a deep breath, Jayne pushed the visual and gazed upon Ed Garrett for the first time in almost ten years.

Her jaw dropped in surprise when she saw him. Before her was a stranger, only vaguely reminiscent of the youth she had known and loved. He had matured and changed, but his dark eyes and wide, sensuous mouth remained the same. Slivers of gray shot through his dark hair, surprising in one still so young. Ironically Ed had gained weight. The buttons of his jacket strained against a bulging waistline. Gone was the trim physique of a high-school athlete. In its place was a thicker, less attractive figure.

Poking the button to admit him, Jayne smiled slightly, the smile of a predator about to pounce. The tables had turned. She was in the position of power now, and she could sense it flowing through her veins. All thoughts of Chad and his church fled as she flung open the apartment door and welcomed Ed to meet his nemesis.

"Jaynie! Jaynie Lindstrom! It's good to see . . ." Ed's words trailed away as he took in the sight before him. Statuesque and regal, Jayne met him, her slender hand extended in a cool but pleasant greeting. Her eyes flickered with hidden thoughts, adding to her mystery and allure.

"Hello, Ed. It's been a long time. Do come in." Aloof, but with charm, Jayne played the game as she had so often imagined it, confounding the man with her apparent disinterest and kindling in him a raging desire to reclaim what he had cast aside.

Stumbling on the threshold of the door, Ed trudged into the room, still stunned by the vision before him.

"Sit there—in the lounge chair. It's the most comfortable. Would you care for a Perrier with a twist of lime? Or a diet drink, perhaps? Since I attempt to carry the Body Images program over into my personal life, I can't offer you anything stronger."

"Whatever that was with the lime is okay for me. Soda pop isn't much my style."

You haven't much style anymore, Ed, was the venomous thought that came to Jayne's mind, but she smiled graciously and prepared his drink.

"Well, I must say, you're not the same little Plain Jayne we used to have so much fun teasing! You're a real knock-out now!"

Fun! Fun for whom? she wondered. *How can inflicting pain be fun?*

Aloud, she answered, "I don't remember those days as especially enchanting, Ed. Particularly your part in them."

"I'm sorry, Jayne. You got a shabby deal from me. I'd like to make it up to you." He looked regretful, troubled by the memories of his callous youth.

Unsure if he had come planning to say those words, or had just decided at the door, Jayne still toyed with him, holding him at bay.

"Your apology is quite sufficient. I want nothing from you."

30

Stymied by her remarks, Ed began to squirm in his seat. He had obviously planned to come as a conquering hero, ready to thrill a lost and lonely girl. Jayne could see he was not at all prepared for what he had found.

Tink-tink-tink. Two pairs of eyes flew to the visual screen by the door, both grateful for the interruption.

Gliding to the screen, Jayne smiled as she viewed Chad's familiar form clad in a running suit. Huffing and sweating, he waved into the security camera before he jogged through the door Jayne opened for him.

Momentarily he was at her door, pounding and yodeling to be let in.

"Hi! Want to go running? The evening is perfect. . . . Excuse me. Am I interrupting something?" Chad's perpetual motion ground to a halt at the sight of Ed Garrett ensconced in the pillowy sectional surrounded by shimmering candles.

"No, not at all, Chad, I'm delighted to see you!" Sincerity rang out in Jayne's voice. Only Ed's narrowing eyes held irritation and resentment.

"Chad, this is Ed Garrett. An . . . ahem . . . acquaintance from the past. Ed, Chad Richards, my business partner and dear friend."

Chad raised an eyebrow in surprise at his elevation in position since this morning.

Ed struggled up from the pillows to a standing position and stuck out a slightly beefy hand toward Chad. The younger man towered over him.

31

"Nice to meet you. Jayne and I go way back . . . way, way back," he emphasized. "It's good to see her again." He leveled his gaze at Chad, implying that he had staked out his territory long ago, and that Chad was not to trespass.

Jayne could feel the tension spark between the two men. They appeared to be facing off in some primeval battle she did not fully understand.

Intentionally shattering the heavy mood, she playfully stamped a dainty foot and announced, "As much as I have enjoyed seeing both of you, I'll have to ask you to leave now."

As both heads, one dark and one fair, turned to her in astonishment, she continued, "I didn't get my book work done at the club this morning as I usually do on Sunday, so I am planning to be at work unusually early tomorrow. Therefore, I need my sleep. Thank you for coming by, Chad, Ed. It was delightful to see you both."

With that, she ushered them—both speechless at their dismissal—out the door. It was Chad who recovered first. Sensing what was going on and willing to aid and abet it, he took her face between both hands and kissed her gently, tenderly on the lips, his palms caressing her cheeks. Then flicking a playful finger at a stray lock of silken hair, he walked away whistling, leaving Ed to stand between the closing apartment door and the gaping jaws of the elevator.

Inside, Jayne leaned against the door, legs trembling, head pressed back against the wooden panel. She had done it. She had shown Ed Garrett what he had missed and how little she cared for what and who he was. Why then was her heart still so heavy and devoid of joy? She had waited for almost ten years for this moment. But it was, at best, bittersweet.

The offices of the Body Images Health Club were silent when Jayne slipped through the delivery entrance at 6:00 A.M. the next morning. When filled with people, the noise was gratifying in the long halls. Now empty, her footsteps ricocheted off the concrete walls like machine-gun fire, making her wince as she made her way to her large, tastefully appointed office at the front of the building.

Relieved to be at her door, she turned the key and stepped into the room. Her office, along with Buddy's and Chad's ran across the front of the second story of the building. They were identical in floor plan, but there the similarities ended. Each of the three had decorated his own office, and, to say the least, the results were as distinctive as the owners.

Jayne glanced around the room with renewed delight. Soft blue couches and love seats clustered in two corners, making cozy conversation pits. White wicker tables and high-backed chairs filled with cushions of the same peach, blue, and white print that graced the walls above white chair rails completed the visiting areas. Lush green plants hung from the ceiling and filled every open space, spilling healthy green foliage across the white wicker. A huge ficus tree dominated one corner of the room, its leaves glinting from the spotlights that Jayne flipped on as she entered the room.

Her feet sank into the pale peach carpet, plush and deep, and she kicked off her leather sandals and tossed them into the hidden closet she had designed. Its door whispered shut, closing over the sound equipment that sent continual music flowing throughout the club.

"You're in charge of keeping the place classy, Jayne," Chad had said. So when patrons heard the strains of Tchaikovsky, Beethoven, or Vivaldi lilting through the intercoms, they knew Jayne had chosen the music. On occasion, however, when they were greeted with the pulsating beats of country-western singers or rock groups, Chad or Buddy more likely was responsible.

Chad's office, Jayne knew, was rich with deep cream, navy and burgundy—a combination of masculine elegance and contemporary flair. Behind the massive light oak desk swam a wall of tropical fish—angels, red oscars, silver dollars, and neon tetras—staring, unblinking, into the room. A computer perched atop the gleaming desk, its keyboard and electronics modules, screen, diskette unit and printer overseeing the chrome and glass furniture. Only a well-worn Bible lying on the low coffee table, the pages grayed from thumbing, spoke of the inner man.

Amused at the thought of the vast differences in their tastes, Jayne thought of Buddy's office, vaguely reminiscent of a warehouse gym. Buddy was concerned only that the floor would support his private collection of weights, a complex affair of lifts and pulleys, benches and boards.

A widower, Buddy had decorated his office alone. The industrial-gray carpet was echoed in the walls, the only bright spots in the room being the red vinyl benches of the weight machine. Posters of sleek, posturing weight lifters covered the walls, and stacks of weight-lifting magazines cluttered the corners. An army cot with a deep and precarious sag in the center occupied the middle of the room, an olive drab blanket draped carelessly across it. No matter how Chad and Jayne had teased and chided, Buddy insisted that his office was just as he liked it. "I can sleep, read, and lift weights in it. What more could I want?"

Jayne knew surprisingly little of Buddy's private life"—only that his wife had died, before Jayne came to Body Images, more than six years ago in a tragic motorcycle accident . . ." that had also claimed the life of their young son. Grief-stricken, Buddy had thrown himself into the small business he and his wife had started, building it into the fashionable, money-making health club it was today. All his energies were devoted to Body Images—and to those who needed him.

Jayne knew full well she could not have made it through those first trying weeks if it hadn't been for Buddy's broad, often tear-stained shoulder and listening ear.

He rarely discussed his own problems but was always there for others. *A compassionate listener. That's Buddy.* There were some interesting men in her life, Jayne admitted to herself, more of them now than ever before.

Smiling, Jayne crossed her office to the large wicker bird cage, pulled off its cover and was greeted by a raucous uproar from the pair of pale blue parakeets within.

"Hi, babies. Did you have a good night?" Talking as she fed them, she planned her day.

"First thing I have to do today is all that work I didn't do yesterday. Taking Sundays off just won't work for me!" With that, she slipped into a pair of court shoes and headed for the front desk to set up the week's schedule.

By the time Chad arrived, Jayne was deeply immersed in outlines for the nutrition seminars. Padding in on soft-soled shoes, Chad stood before her quietly, a questioning look in his eyes. It was some moments before Jayne sensed his presence and looked up to meet the inquiring green gaze. She could read the questions there: *What's going on? Who is Ed Garrett?* The questions were plain, but before he could utter them, three men in shorts and T-shirts came along, laughing and joking.

"Hey, Chad! Earl and I think we can whip you and Marv in a quick game before league play starts. How about it?" Clapping a thick arm around Chad's broad shoulders, the man led him away, assuming acquiescence.

Chad went along with them, but twisted his head back to look toward Jayne. She could see the concern and confusion in those expressive eyes, but try as she would, she could not meet them.

She knew Chad would never approve of her plans, but Ed Garrett had to pay for the way he had treated her. She wanted to savor the sweetness of her revenge. She'd suffered most of

36

her adult life with the vision of herself—undesirable and plain—that Ed had left her. Now it was time for him to pay for that youthful, thoughtless cruelty.

And he *would* regret leaving her. For she had metamorphasized into something worth having, a rare and lovely butterfly that would hover tantalizingly just out of reach, freed at last from its chrysalis.

Absorbed by her scheme to lead Ed on to his ultimate disappointment, she turned back to her work. Shortly she heard the sound of voices arguing volubly.

"No, you may not join by the week! Our trial membership is four months and that's that! Our policy is set and you'll have to abide by it if you are seriously interested in joining Body Images Health Club." Buddy's rumbling voice was unusually stern and there was more than a hint of anger in it.

"That's ridiculous! I'm not going to be here for four months! Why should I spend all that money and have it go to waste? Surely you must have *some* influence around here! And if you don't, I do. I'm a friend of one of the proprietors, Jayne Lindstrom!"

As the owners of the voices came into view, Jayne recognized trouble immediately. Genial, gentle Buddy, normally slow to anger, was hunched into a glowering position, thick neck buried deep in his broad shoulders. His face was red and mottled. Pompous and cocksure, Ed Garrett strutted beside him, chipping away at Buddy's logic.

"You *must* have a program for people who only want to use the facilities for a few weeks! If not, that's very poor planning, if you ask me!"

"We didn't ask you, mister. Four months is our shortest membership. We feel that one can't benefit from our programs in less time."

"Well, in four months, just about *any* program could work!"

Jayne cut in just before Buddy let loose with some colorful opinions of his own.

"I'll take care of this, Buddy, thank you." She stood and smiled warmly at her husky friend. Easygoing and amiable as Buddy normally was, Ed must have worked hard to get him into such a state.

Rolling his eyes in mock horror, Buddy gladly washed his hands of the whole encounter, pushing his palms through the air as if to shove the problem onto his partner's shoulders. He lumbered off toward the weight room, where Jayne knew he'd vent the steam Ed's prima donna behavior had generated.

"Really, Ed! Was that necessary?" Softly chiding, Jayne continued, "Buddy is my partner in this enterprise. Did you need to badger him so?"

"Your partner? That big lug? Why he doesn't look like he has the brains!" Ed did not notice the tightness etched around Jayne's rosy lips, nor the cold light that formed in her eyes.

Jayne spoke quietly, but her voice was heavy with meaning. "Please do not judge people by their looks, Ed. It's both cruel and inaccurate. Buddy is a fine man and a dear friend." She put her pen down with such force that even Ed looked at her askance as her long fingernails snapped against the laminated counter.

"Now, then." Suddenly amiable, Jayne suppressed her anger and turned the subject back to the club and her ultimate plan. "If you wish to join Body Images for less than four months, perhaps something can be arranged." Outwardly poised, she took charge, leaving Ed to stammer out his explanations.

"Well, I'm here on business for five or six weeks, eight at the most, and I thought that it would be a good chance to get in shape," he patted his thick middle fondly, "and at the same time, renew my acquaintance with you, Jayne."

She could not have asked for a more opportune turn of events. With Ed in such close proximity and so eager to resume their earlier relationship, Jayne could lead him on until she tired of the game—and teach him once and for all how deeply he had hurt her.

CHAPTER FOUR

FLOWERS . . . AGAIN. For the fifth time in the weeks since Ed had joined the health club, Jayne found flowers on her desk. Arranged with meticulous care and a studious eye for balance and design, they reflected the professionalism of the florist down the street. Beautiful as they were, Jayne somehow longed for another bouquet like the one she had once received from Chad—purchased on a whim from a street vendor and tumbling gaily from their green paper wrap. There had been love in those posies. All she could sense in these was great expense and a depressing, funereal smell.

Picking a red-tipped carnation from the arrangement, Jayne held it to her nose, sniffed, and wrinkled her face in disgust. She'd never liked the smell of carnations. Tossing it aside, she paced behind the desk, restless and edgy. She couldn't even enjoy a flower since she'd embarked on this vengeful crusade of hers.

She wished desperately that Ed would quit nagging her about Chad. He seemed to be attacking her partner on every front. Ed had been adamant earlier.

"You shouldn't be so chummy with that business partner of yours, Jayne. Bad company politics. I see the way he looks at you. Don't encourage him! If you two have a tiff, the business suffers."

Jayne had brushed aside his irritating comments, but Ed had put his finger on a raw nerve. The fear was legitimate. Her dream for Body Images was all she had. She would do nothing to jeopardize it.

She sniffed in derision at her own thoughts. It was painful to reflect on a life empty of all but a business. *I've wasted my life so far. What's left?*

"You're just jealous, Ed. That's all!" She said aloud to the flowers on her desk. She poked a lacquered nail at the petals.

Ed had been chipping away at Chad for days, labeling him "the big, dumb jock" until she could not understand how Chad could take the badgering so graciously.

Still, in other ways, Ed was trying. The restaurants he chose for their evenings together were lovely; the plays, entertaining. Even she had to admit their last date had been delightful.

She smiled at the memory. The quaint dinner theater was a place Jayne had always wanted to go but never had, hesitant to make reservations for a table for one and even more reluctant to infringe on her friends' time at home with their families by asking someone to join her. Her aversion to singles' bars and her compulsion for work had left her uncomfortable with casual dating. Suitors had persisted, but Jayne never allowed a man more than an evening or two before she began refusing his company.

Driving up to the building only reminded her of how secluded she had become. She had set a rigid pattern of behavior, closing out any attempts at intimacy, brooding on her frustrating past. She had been glad for the opportunity to visit the amazing little theater which drew crowds that each week numbered more than the population of the entire town.

Surprised by the theater's size, they had explored the ramps and stairs leading to the four theaters and large lounges. Somehow, someway, Ed's hand had found its way around Jayne's burgandy nails. Laughingly they tossed pennies into an artificial pool, making wishes. Jayne's casual verbal wishes did not echo the ones her mind was screaming.

She could still remember the playful banter.

"Make a wish, Jayne. I'm almost out of coins. Make these count!" Ed dribbled copper and silver into her outstretched palm.

"Three wishes? Is that all I get?" Jayne moved her free finger across the glinting lucre. "Then I wish for the success of Body Images!" The coin splashed into the acquamarine pond and settled to the bottom. "And, and . . ." Jayne racked her brain. She could not repeat the words marching through her mind. "And a tasty meal and a pleasant evening!" Quickly, she threw in the last two, anxious to be rid of them.

As they drifted to the bottom, she canceled her verbal wishes with a fervent mental one: *Chad ... Chad ... Chad. ...* "Seems to me you wasted some good wishes, Jayne. Since I only need one, I'm going to make it good. And I think you know what it will be !" Ed turned toward her with a gleam in his eye.

Jayne inhaled sharply, not wanting to hear his wish, knowing it would somehow involve her in ways that could never be.

Just as the coin arced in the air, a waitress tugged on Ed's shoulder, telling them that their table was ready. The coin settled with the wish unspoken, and Jayne vowed she would not let the conversation drift that way again. She would have to reveal her plan too early if Ed turned his thoughts toward marriage. She was not done toying with him yet. . . . So far she had missed the pleasure in her plan and she was determined to find it.

Having only picked at her dinner, Jayne allowed the waitress to remove her plate. Irritated by her apparent disinterest, Ed chided her.

"You barely touched your food! What's wrong?"

"I had plenty, Ed."

"Since when is two carrots and four bites of a twelve-ounce prime rib plenty?"

"It's enough for me. Please, Ed. I don't criticize the way you eat."

"That's because I *do* eat. Are you sure it's worth it?"

Jayne studied him from under half-closed lids. She had often asked herself that question. She was never more sure of the answer. It *was* worth it, for Ed Garrett was once again sitting across from her, solicitous and caring, being primed for his fall.

Ironically the play was about marriage, its ups and downs, its pains and pleasures. In a tender moment onstage, Ed's hand crept possessively over hers. She could feel the warm, hard metal of his ring grating against her knuckle in a proprietary grip. His warm skin sent a shiver of apprehension through her.

Alarmed and frightened by the insinuating gesture, Jayne, inexperienced and unsophisticated in these matters, pulled back, moving her chair away from his. Undaunted, Ed edged nearer, refusing to release his grasp on her.

Then, surprisingly, he let go of her hand. Patting it gently he laid it back in her lap as if returning it to her possession. He had not pressed further, and the night ended on a casual, light-hearted note.

Ed had grown, matured. The blustering pomposity surfaced occasionally, but his manners for the most part were impeccable. He treated her as if she were a queen, ushering her through crowds, shielding her from the crush with his body, pulling out chairs with a embarrassing flair. Oh, Ed was impressive, all right. But she'd seen him this way before—with the girl he left her for so many years earlier.

"Jayne! I see my flowers arrived!" Ed appeared, shattering her reflective mood. But he seemed so open and eager that Jayne couldn't help returning his smile as he came toward the front desk, dragging a bulging duffle bag, sneakers tied together by the laces and draped around his neck.

"You really shouldn't have, Ed. They're lovely, though. Thank you." Remaining cool and keeping her distance, she avoided looking his way as she spoke. She knew her apparent disinterest would frustrate him further.

"Is that all you can say—'thank you?' I spent an hour picking them out, telling the florist just how I wanted them!" Unspoken emotion played on Ed's swarthy face. He was obviously not accustomed to having his romantic overtures taken so lightly.

"Thank you again, Ed. For your time as well." She could see the look of irritation cross his face. He had been trying so desperately to please her. In fact, it had been difficult not to respond to his lavish attention. Gregarious and puppy-like, Ed could have been very endearing . . . under different circumstances.

Breaking down slightly, she put one rose-tipped nail to his jaw, following the hard line to his chin. Smiling then, she said softly and sincerely, "You've been very generous, Ed. More than you should be."

Disengaging her gaze from Ed's rapt one, she glanced over his shoulder toward the hall only to see Chad staring at them, his shoulders drooping at the intimate scene.

His green eyes round and swimming with pain, Jayne could read the hurt and confusion crossing

45

Chad's even features. As he backed away, Chad bumped into Buddy just leaving his office, weight lifter's manual in hand.

Buddy glanced up to see why the imperturbable Chad was fleeing. Jayne could read fury in his pale eyes, and she cringed slightly, saddened that she could not reveal to her dear friends what she was doing. They would have to think the worst of her, then—that she could dismiss the gentle, lovable Chad for whatever it was she saw in Ed Garrett, the man who had wounded her so.

Sending a pleading glance Buddy's way, Jayne's look begged forgiveness. In return she received an icy stare of disgust just before Buddy clamped a burly arm around Chad's shoulders and led him off down the hall in the opposite direction.

Jayne's heart constricted as she watched the two trek down the hall. Chad stumbled once while his husky friend supported him, talking fervently into his ear. Jayne's cheeks burned at the thought of what he might be saying. She was beginning to hate this charade more and more with each day that passed.

Ed, encouraged by the not unsuccessful evening at the theater with Jayne, became bolder and more creative in his pursuit. One day he appeared at lunch time, bearing a woven picnic basket full of French bread, paté de foie gras, and sumptuous tree-ripened fruits.

"What do you think you're doing?" Buddy met him at the door, arms bent, hand on hips.

"None of your business, old man. This is for

Jayne." Ed brushed past the human wall, bumping Buddy in the thigh with the cumbersome basket.

With a beefy hand applied to one shoulder, Buddy stopped Ed's progress midstream. "If it's Jayne's business, it's mine—here at the club, anyway."

"I'm bringing her a surprise, okay? Lunch. She never wants to go out at noon, so I thought I'd bring something special in. Does that meet with your approval?" Ed's voice dripped with sarcasm.

The meaty hand dropped away. Jayne had been losing weight again. If Ed could persuade her to eat, it would be a blessing. Jayne had even quit confiding in Buddy, once her closest confidant. She had erected a cool, protective wall around herself, creating a puzzle no one at Body Images seemed able to solve. Ed was the key to the puzzle, but so far the pieces didn't fit.

"Ed! What are you lugging around?" Jayne poked her head from her office and spied the basket tied with a red ribbon.

"Lunch! I went to the deli and asked for the classiest picnic menu they could recommend, and here it is!" He held the basket up for her inspection, gripping the handle with both hands.

Shaking her head, Jayne waved him into the office. As she turned to go, Ed gave Buddy a triumphant grin before he followed her inside.

"Now, let's see what's in here . . . bread, paté, fruit. How thoughtful! I didn't realize I was hungry, but perhaps I will eat a bite or two!"

Spreading the checkered paper tablecloth over

the coffee table, Jayne withdrew paper plates and arranged the delicacies. Sitting cross-legged on the floor, she nibbled on a crust of bread spread with the delicate pate. Ed, entranced with her graceful movements, followed every gesture, forgetting to eat.

"What are you staring at?"

The question surprised him. He had forgotten himself.

"You, Jayne. I was just thinking how much you had changed since we first knew each other . . . I mean . . . well . . . if you'd been . . . maybe things would have been different. . . ."

Even Ed was startled by the hostility that flickered across Jayne's features.

"Thanks for the lunch, Ed. Gotta go."

With that, Jayne unfolded herself from her sitting position and walked out of the office, leaving Ed alone on the floor in front of the gaily appointed table, a crust of bread in one hand, a pear in the other, and a mystified expression on his face.

CHAPTER FIVE

A TENUOUS, UNSPOKEN PACT developed between the three owners of Body Images Health Club as the tense days of Ed Garrett's membership passed. Unwilling and unable to defend her actions, Jayne slipped quietly from one duty to another, hoping not to meet Buddy's baleful glare or Chad's inquisitive looks.

Buddy, having taken an immediate and intense dislike to Ed, spent a good share of this time avoiding him entirely in the long corridors, popping in and out of rooms if he saw Ed coming. In the moments when they did come face-to-face, he was obviously suppressing his irritation with Ed's very presence at the club.

Chad apparently felt none of the guilt or anger of his partners and was able to carry on almost normally, pleasant and uncomplaining. But he was unable to conceal the injured, bemused

49

looks that crossed his face whenever he saw Jayne and Ed together.

Jayne, looking particularly fresh and alluring in a teal blue body stocking and teal and white striped leg warmers, met Ed slipping in the back entrance, dragging the inevitable duffel bag.

"Well, you're here early today! All your sales meetings over already?" She greeted him with the small, cool smile she had cultivated for his benefit, amused by the sight of Ed so intent on his progress.

Nodding, Ed answered, "I'll be here earlier from now on. Things are winding down. I have a few weeks left, but the big push is past. Now I'll be able to spend more time with you."

Emotions battled across Jayne's countenance. She wanted Ed to leave; but she needed him to stay. Although she hated the uncomfortable atmosphere at the club, the perverse muse would not rest. She could not seem to give up her vindictive plan. She'd waited years to see Ed Garrett squirm . . . now was her chance.

Suddenly an idea occurred to her. "Ed! Come with me to my exercise class! It starts in fifteen minutes, so there's plenty of time for you to change."

"Aw, that's only for women. What would I do in there?"

"Well, it just so happens that there are several men in this class. I've been promoting my classes to the male members of Body Images for so long that I think some of them finally decided to try it just to show me up!" Jayne wanted Ed in that class, needed him there. She had a point to make.

"Well, you can hardly expect men to enjoy all those silly dancing exercises you women do!"

Smiling knowingly, Jayne responded, "You may be surprised by some of our 'silly dancing exercises.' They are considerably more grueling than you might realize. Anyway, I'm going to concentrate on stretching and bending in this class. Some of the men are going to use it as their warm-up for handball and squash. Interested?"

Unwilling, but unable to ignore the challenge, Ed finally agreed. "Okay, but if I get bored, I'm not coming back!"

"You won't be bored, I'll guarantee that!"

Entering the large mirrored studio, Jayne greeted her students warmly. Friends all, most had been members of Body Images since its inception and made up an enthusiastic fan club.

Waving to the men in the back row, she greeted them specifically. "I'm delighted to begin a coed class today. You men haven't been giving us much credit for our physical fitness endeavors, so we're glad to have you here to show you just how tough we women are!" She could hear Ed sniffing in derision near her shoulder.

"Well, let's get at it then!" joked a deep voice in the back row.

"All right. Take your places, please. Here we go!"

Gone was the soft, sweet Jayne, replaced by an unrelenting drill sergeant, barking orders into the air over the contemporary beat emitted by the tape recorder.

"Let's loosen up with some side stretches. Don't bounce, just stretch. We want to increase flexibility, not injure muscles." Jayne waved from side to side slowly and gracefully, like a willow in the wind, giving instructions as she moved. The class followed, some derisive snorts and hoots coming from the back row.

"Breathe deeply now—get that oxygen into your bloodstream—clean out those toxins!"

Jayne kept one eye on the wall of mirrors before her, reflecting all the activity taking place in the room. She noticed a sneer beginning to curl Ed's lip.

Knowing that would be easy to remedy, Jayne called, "Now a hamstring stretch. Think of putting your chest on your knees and your buttocks on the ceiling."

She folded herself in half, grasping her ankles with her hands and placing her nose to her calves, remaining in this folded-double position as she continued her instructions. "We have over six hundred muscles in our bodies, we're just working on a few! Come on, guys—let's get rid of that spare tire!"

She could see Ed struggling in the mirror, his ankles remaining precariously out of reach of his hands unless he squatted slightly, bending his knees. His nose came nowhere near his calves. Even the hooting in the back row had subsided.

But Jayne had just begun. Firing directions as she demonstrated, she had the class take a new position. "Feet apart in a wide stance, now. Bend your knees. Touch your left elbow to your

52

right knee and your right elbow to your left knee." She swung easily from side to side.

"All right, now touch your *ankle* with your elbow for a better stretch." She demonstrated, her left leg straight out to her side and left elbow touching her right ankle; her right arm stretched high in the air over her head. Her luxuriant hair, clasped into a half-moon clip, cascaded over one shoulder. The catcalls were replaced by groans and shudders as the class endeavored to imitate the lissome instructor.

"Now everyone should be warmed up. Let's go on to some more difficult exercises."

The hoots had stopped, but there were some audible moans emanating from the back of the room. Ed and several others were still trying to extricate themselves from the last position. Placing his hands flat on the floor, Ed hoisted himself from a squatting position to a standing one in time to see Jayne slide gracefully to the floor for a grueling twenty minutes of what she called "abdominals."

Buddy, watching from the observation deck, grinned in the half-light. Jayne was really giving them a workout today. Funny she'd do that to Ed . . . unless . . . she *wanted* to.

The music and Jayne's instructions pulsed on, in staccato time. "Keep your elbows back as you sit up—pull with those abdominals! Now, on your back, legs in the air. Then sit up, extending your arms through your legs. . ."

Jayne noticed the hour ticking away. She eased into a sitting position for a moment to ask, "Had enough for today?" Knowing their answer, she

53

voiced it: "Let's cool down!" Glancing at the red, intense faces, she smiled slightly.

She remembered attending her first exercise classes here at Body Images. Coming out of the dressing room in that first baggy gray warm-up suit of hers had seemed strenuous enough. Self-conscious, embarrassed, ashamed of her looks, she had stayed in the far corner, as far away from the mirrors and instructor as she could get. But she had endured the pain of aching muscles and personal humiliation to get to this point. Now it seemed worth it all to see Ed struggling and winded, while she was limber and barely stressed after a vigorous hour.

She led the group into a stretching cool-down. "Sit on the floor with your legs extended and in an open position. Bend to the left side and touch your left foot with your right hand, while your left hand is placed on your right inner thigh. Repeat to the other side. Here we go!"

Jayne sat, legs extended out to her sides at ninety-degree angles to her body, bending gracefully from one side to the other. Then she moved her feet together, legs straight in front, and lowered her head to her knees, grasping her ankles and holding the position as she listened to the groaning behind her.

Inhaling deeply, she raised her head and looked around the room. Most of the women, familiar with Jayne's routines from other classes, were laughing and chatting as they draped their towels around their necks and headed for the pink and silver shower room. The men, particularly Ed, were more subdued, glancing at Jayne's sleek body with something akin to awe.

Ed, with beads of perspiration coating his face, approached her on what appeared to be very watery legs and with new respect in his eyes. "How do you do that, anyway?"

"Hours and months of hard, grueling work, Ed. And," she added almost inaudibly, "I have you to thank for it." Turning from Ed, she left the mirrored room, her slender teal reflection shimmering back to him.

Jogging lightly down the hallway was Chad in crisp, navy blue shorts and a navy and white striped T-shirt, two-pound weights strapped to his ankles.

"Hi, stranger!" he called to Jayne. His even teeth gleamed in the tan face, echoing the white stripe of his shirt. He paused, jogging in place, to talk to Jayne. The biceps in his arms bulged as he flexed them.

Tugging nervously at the fleecy white towel around her neck, she smiled and thought, *Dear Chad, always the same, no matter how badly I treat him*. Aloud, she ventured, "Did we put in a jogging track when I wasn't looking?"

"An excellent idea! Let's consider it. Then I wouldn't have to prowl the halls and alleys to get my miles in. Actually, I agreed to play in the tournament next week, and I thought I'd better get in shape."

"You've never been out of shape, Chad," Jayne retorted, eyes following the strong, smooth muscles of his legs from the hem of his shorts to the weights at his ankles.

"Glad you think so. I could say the same thing about you."

"But we both know better, don't we, Chad?" Her question was pointed, bitter.

Unwilling to pursue that conversation, Chad changed topics. "I hear from Buddy that you gave that new coed class quite a workout. The guys won't be joking about ladies' sissified exercise classes any more!"

"Almost everyone has had some experience with aerobics, so I thought we'd jump right in. Besides, sometimes a challenge is nice." She answered nonchalantly, trying to divert his line of questioning. Chad was coming precariously close to knowing why that class had been given such a workout.

"Throwing down the gauntlet, so to speak?" Casually asked, the question was fraught with meaning. The challenge had been for Ed. How could Chad know that?

Jayne knew he was wondering why she had begun to invest so much of her time in Ed, but Chad wouldn't push. Sweet Chad. If only Ed hadn't come along. If only she weren't devoting so much of her self to seeking revenge. If only she weren't continually confronted by Chad's presence. Realizing the fruitlessness of "if onlys," she mentally shook herself from her reverie in time to hear Chad asking, "How about a power-packed protein punch? I've got the fixin's in my office?"

"Oh, Chad, not one of those horrible gray milk

shakes with seaweed and who knows what else in it?'' Her face wrinkled in mock disgust.

"Nope, I got a new recipe. Come on!"

Tugging the reluctant Jayne by the hand, he pulled her into the plush cave of his office. Switching on recessed lights and pulling back the wall that concealed his private mini-kitchen, Chad started concocting the brew.

"This has carob in it. Good as chocolate— drowns the taste of the seaweed. Just kidding!'' The patter went on as he measured and dumped ingredients into the blender. Discovering a little of this or a dab of that in the canisters on the shelf, he'd carefully measure the amount he needed, put it into the machine and then with a "what's the difference" attitude, dump the contents of the entire container in as well.

Jayne was laughing hysterically by the time he turned the machine on, whizzing the mixture into a fatal gray color.

"I thought you promised that this wouldn't be gray!''

"Well, I didn't think it would! And I followed the recipe so carefully, too!''

Winking grandly, he pulled out two crystal tumblers and poured the ooze into them, garnishing each with a sprig of parsley.

"Parsley, Chad! Yuk!''

"Well, I bought it at the market this morning for the lady next door. I stuck it in my refrigerator and it's the closest I can come to chocolate shavings and whipped cream. Pretend it's seaweed.''

Laughing, Jayne wrinkled her nose in preparation and took a tiny sip of the concoction. "Why, it's actually good! How did you do that?"

Pretending to flip things into the blender, Chad responded, "It's all in the wrist. If you play racquetball, you can do this . . . *if* you have the recipe!"

"Well, I never thought I'd be saying this, but I think *I'd* like the recipe. Please?" Jayne gave him her most sweetly pleading look, holding the glass of gray mixture next to her face. Parsley appeared to be growing out of one ear.

"Nope. It's my tenuous hold on you, Jayne. You'll have to come to me every time you want one—day or night."

She stood up suddenly, breaking the light-hearted moment, now contemplative. Chad seemed to be saying that he wanted to be back in her life. But she also realized that he would not interfere in her relationship with Ed.

Why is it working out like this? she wondered. For the first time since Ed left her, she had found a man she could love—a man who would return that love. But now she had entrenched herself in a scheme from which there seemed no escape.

Wandering around the room, gently moving her fingers over chrome and glass, she paused at the coffee table. Dropping onto the burgundy sectional, she picked up the well-worn Testament lying there.

"You read this a lot, don't you, Chad?"

"Every day—more than once." He smiled lazily from the reclining position he had taken at his desk, feet propped up on top of papers, chair tilted backward. "You have one, don't you?"

58

"I suppose I must, somewhere. Everyone does. I mean, isn't it rather like a dictionary—a must for every household, whether you use it or not?" She flipped through the pages, skimming, but not really seeing.

"It's a must for every *life*, Jayne. I have several, if you want to borrow one."

"Maybe sometime, thanks." She meandered toward the wall of tropical fish and stood watching them glide silently through the water. "Fish are rather peaceful, don't you think? They just cut through the water, sailing along." She stood dreamy-eyed before the tank, watching a huge angelfish watching her.

"I'm peaceful, Jayne—and *I'm* not a fish."

Startled back from the watery depths, she turned to look at him. It was true. He was more at peace with himself than any other person she had ever met. She wondered idly where such serenity came from.

As if reading her thoughts, Chad asked, "There's a guest speaker tonight at the little church we went to. Would you like to go? There's special music and Bessie Norheim has been asking me why I haven't brought you back. She wants to get to know you better."

Jayne smiled fondly at the thought of the little white-haired woman. She was a honey, no doubt about that. Maybe it would be fun to spend an evening with Chad and look for some of that peace he radiated.

The jarring buzz of the intercom startled them both. Chad swung his long legs off the desk and punched the audio button. Buddy's deep voice came booming across the line: "Is Jayne in there? This Garrett fellow has been looking for her, and he's making himself a pain in the neck! I sent him to the whirlpool."

Disappointed by the unwelcome intrusion, the two looked at each other, Chad's eyes inquiring, Jayne's sad. She laid a hand on his broad shoulder, squeezed it gently, and started out of the room, turning back to say softly, "Thanks for the milk shake. I'll remember where I got it if I need another."

Chad nodded briefly, and began to page through the worn Bible Jayne had laid down on his desk.

Jayne quickly changed into a black maillot and padded for the whirlpool to see what Ed wanted. She had wrapped herself in a striped black and white caftan for the trek down the hall. Entering the steaming tub room, she saw Ed, submerged but for his head, in the bubbling pool.

Struggling to sit in the roiling waters, a look of pain crossed Ed's reddened face. "How can you still walk after that workout you gave us this morning?" He winced as he got a handhold on the side of the tub and pulled himself upright.

"Why, Ed. I normally teach three classes a day! Yours was just the start! I haven't even broken a sweat yet." The exaggeration was worth seeing the downcast look on Ed's face. It was delightful to remind him just who was in top physical form now.

Dropping the billowing caftan to the floor, she stood before him, kicking off her thongs. Ed looked at her, increasingly aware of the lean, lissome beauty of the woman he had once jilted. Her long legs were like those of a finely honed racing filly, sleek and molded.

Before either had a chance to speak, Chad came padding in as well, muscles rippling in his bare chest, towel draped around his neck.

"Thought I'd join you for a soak in the whirlpool. Do you mind?"

"Not a bit!" Jayne was secretly delighted to know that Chad had followed her. "Shall we both join Ed?"

The two beautiful bodies slid into the water, laughing and teasing, as Ed sank slightly lower, unwilling to expose any more of his flabby, winter-white skin than necessary.

Too soon for Jayne, the intercom buzzed and Buddy's voice drifted down to them, "Long distance, Chad. Some supplier wants you right away!"

"Thanks, Bud. Be right there!"

Climbing out of the water, Chad mopped himself with a towel, flung it around his shoulders, and left the room, waving back toward the two still soaking.

Left alone, Jayne and Ed stared at each other wordlessly. The uneasy silence lasted some moments. Jayne allowed her fingers to caress the surface of the water as she searched for threads of conversation.

"I believe it's time for me to get back to work. I have another exercise class and a nutrition seminar to get to. How about you, Ed?"

Jayne suspected that he was not yet comfortable exposing his untoned body to her clinical inspection, so she was not surprised when he shook his head.

"Not just yet," he said predictably.

He would probably not leave the bubbling waters until she was gone. Obliging him, Jayne pulled herself out of the pool in one fluid motion, threw her caftan around her, and left without a backward glance.

Dried and dressed in a pale blue leotard and legwarmers, Jayne noticed Ed scribbling furiously on the clipboards at the front desk. Curious, she waited until he disappeared through the front door before investigating.

To her surprise Ed's name appeared in several places on the sign-up lists: racquetball lessons, her exercise class, and even weight lifting. Buddy would love that!

Smiling to herself, she strolled back down the hall. Perhaps Ed was beginning to experience some of the self-consciousness that had plagued her all the years of her life.

CHAPTER SIX

RESTLESS AND AT ODDS WITH HERSELF, Jayne felt little like returning to her apartment. Even though she had purposefully avoided Ed, she didn't relish the thought of empty rooms. Once her haven, now its lonely confines smothered her with silence.

Jayne idly wished now that she had encouraged the occasional friendly overtures of her neighbors. But, wrapped as she had been in her shroud of insecurity, she had shrugged off their welcome, feeling sure that sooner or later they would find her dull, disappointing, unlovable. She had held everyone at bay. Growing more and more beautiful externally had not solved her interior strife.

Tonight she was desperately lonely; she craved companionship. It was Chad with whom she wanted to spend her evening. But she dared not approach him with such a request. Were he to refuse, as she was afraid he might, it would be far too devastating to her fragile ego.

Instead, she slipped behind the wheel of her sleek little car and pulled onto the freeway, heading for the center of town. Following Interstate 35W, she drove toward the black-glass IDS Tower, looming fifty-seven stories over the city, dwarfing the once impressive Foshay Tower. Over two million people lived in this sprawling metropolis, but Jayne felt as isolated as if she were whizzing to the Arctic Circle.

Zigzagging through the downtown streets, she caught glimpses of the brightly lit Nicollet Mall curving through the downtown area. The skyway system of pedestrian bridges crisscrossed the streets interconnecting the buildings. Tiny figures high above her bustled from place to place.

Driving by the Hubert H. Humphrey Metrodome, Jayne spied a young family strolling down the wide street. Looking up at the skyline and pointing eagerly was a small, chubby girl clutching her mother's hand. The child was dressed in a navy sailor dress with a starched white collar, and glossy black patent leather shoes with white anklets. Dark, thick braids draped over each shoulder. Swinging at the end of each silky rope was a tiny red ribbon.

A wave of nostalgia swept Jayne. She could still remember her first trip to Minneapolis as a stocky, dark-haired child dressed in *her* Sunday best. That "best" had been a thin cotton dress, made from one of her mother's dresses, and with all the style of the feed sacks her father regularly carried from his rickety pickup into the barn. Her

64

sturdy brown shoes, which served for everyday as well as dress, enclosed once-white stockings, clean but grayed by numerous washings.

Plain Jayne, Plain Jayne, can't fit on a train....

How she had hated her growing-up years! The scars appeared to be healed, but, beneath the surface remained festering wounds that were poisoning her life.

Hunger gnawing at her insides, Jayne shook the melancholy thoughts from her mind and set her thoughts toward supper. The small bowl of plain yogurt and diced fresh fruit that she had breakfasted on were no longer sustaining her. She needed something more substantial.

Wishing for an interesting place to dine, she headed for the cobblestone streets of old St. Anthony and St. Anthony Main. Entering one door of the restored limestone building, she was captivated by two white-faced mimes busily climbing an imaginary staircase, graceful and catlike, but feigning exhaustion as the flight of illusory steps continued unendingly. Entranced by their fluid, expressive movements, Jayne settled on the edge of a bench and watched their antics.

She laughed aloud as one tuxedo-suited mimic struggled vainly to free himself from an imaginary box, and the other busied himself polishing a mirror existent only in his mind.

Refreshed by the free-wheeling entertainment, Jayne no longer felt so alone or so hungry. Remembering the small rib-eye steak she had left to thaw, she decided to return to HighTower to eat.

"Jayne! Jayne Lindstrom! Is that you?"

Jayne whirled around at the sound of her name, but there seemed no familiar faces in the sea advancing toward her. Teen-agers, plugged in to earphones and tiny metallic boxes, drifted to their own private, syncopated beat. A gaggle of white heads bobbed toward her as she heard the voice again.

"Jayne! Over here!"

The voice was familiar, but Jayne was not sure where she had heard it. She stood on tiptoe, scanning the crowd, a puzzled look on her face. Startled, she realized the owner of the voice was now standing before her, frail and tiny.

"It's Bessie Norheim. Chad introduced us at church."

Bessie, barely reaching Jayne's shoulder, wore a puckish smile on her face.

"Bessie! How nice to see you again! I couldn't imagine who in the crowd was calling to me!" Jayne was no longer the aloof woman of their prior meeting. She was genuinely delighted to see the warm and friendly little lady.

"That's because I was lost in a sea of white heads! We old ladies all look alike, you know!" Bessie's wry humor was not lost on Jayne. She laughed aloud at the twinkle in Bessie's eye.

"Oh, you do, do you? I think I couldn't find you because you are so short, not so old! Are you out shopping?" Jayne glanced over at the cluster of ladies standing to one side.

"We're celebrating! It's my friend Nora's

seventy-first birthday, and we're taking her out for supper. The twelve of us have celebrated together for years. Each of us happens to have her birthday in a different month, so once a month we go out for dinner. It's become rather a special thing as we have grown older. Some of us don't get out very often, but we always have this evening to look forward to."

"What a wonderful idea! And where are you eating tonight?"

"Well, as we get older, we get more daring. Tonight Nora chose Mexican food. In our younger years, we always went to some nice, reliable steak house, but now we're branching out."

"And exactly what does that mean?" Jayne was delighted by Bessie's youthful attitude. She nearly felt elderly herself by comparison.

"You know—new foods, new places. Chinese, Italian, Greek, German, Polish, Japanese, even pizza! The only thing I've regretted," Bessie's voice lowered to a conspiratorial whisper, "was *sushi*. Her entire face wrinkled into a mask of distaste. "Raw fish, you know."

Jayne could barely suppress the bubbling laughter within her. She could just imagine the little ladies sampling that delicacy!

"I was worried about diseases or worms or something. The waitress assured me it would be fine. I'm still here, so it must have been! But I'm not going back."

"And what restaurant did you pick on your birthday, Bessie?"

"Well, I wanted French, but Martha's birthday

is the month before mine, and she picked that. So, I chose a fast food place."

"Fast food? Really?" Jayne stared at her in amused disbelief.

"Well, my dear, I wanted to know what these teen-agers and young families saw in it. And I must say, I rather enjoyed it, too! Especially the French fries."

"Bessie, you're wonderful!"

"Just trying to keep up with the times, my dear. Now, what are you doing here? Shopping?"

"No, I was just driving around and decided to stop here for something to eat. Then I remembered a steak in my refrigerator, so I was on my way home."

"Will it keep?"

"What?"

"The steak—will it keep? Why don't you join us for dinner?"

"Oh, Bessie, I couldn't! That would be interfering!" Jayne looked longingly at the friendly little woman. It would be wonderful to have her company, but Jayne would force herself on no one.

"We've been eating out once a month for years. It would do us a world of good to have a pretty new face among us. Please, Jayne, I'd like my friends to meet you and vice versa!" Sincerity rang so true in Bessie's voice that Jayne could not resist. "I'd love to, Bessie!"

"Nora, Martha, all of you! Come and meet my friend. She's agreed to dine with us tonight!"

Jayne found herself surrounded by smiling

faces. She would never be able to remember so many names, she thought. Soon she was ushered, in the middle of the group, toward the restaurant.

Finding herself the one most familiar with Mexican foods, Jayne busily described the various dishes and made recommendations.

"I've had tacos, but they were hard to eat. The shells kept crumbling," laughingly complained one little lady.

"Order soft shell tacos. Then you won't have that problem," Jayne suggested.

"Why do they make this sauce so hot?" Nora was waving a hand in front of her mouth after sampling the dip that accompanied a large basket of crispy tortillas.

"Try the mild sauce. I think you dipped into the extra spicy."

"What's a burrito?" That suspicious question came from Bessie. The recent thoughts of *sushi* were still fresh in her mind.

"Try it, Bessie, you'll like it!"

The laughter and chatter went on. Soon two waitresses came, bearing steaming plates of food.

For a moment, after they were served, Jayne found her dark head the only one unbowed in a prayer of thanksgiving. Feeling uncomfortable, she tucked her neck down into her shoulders and glanced furtively from side to side. She didn't know how or for what to pray, and in the sudden hush of reverence, she felt alien, unfit.

Just as quickly as it had occurred, it was over. Warm conversation and laughter surrounded the table. Jayne, now feeling welcome and alive, entered in with a zest she didn't know she possessed, blooming under the easy and total acceptance of the group.

Noticing a sudden furrow in Bessie's brow, Jayne leaned over to inquire, "Is something the matter? You look so worried!"

"I entirely forgot!"

"Forgot what?"

"The birthday cake! It was my turn to order it and I completely forgot. Oh, dear . . . ." Bessie clasped her hands together, wringing them in dismay.

"I'll take care of it, Bessie. Don't worry." Jayne whispered into her friend's ear. Apparently the cake was an important part of their celebrations. Beckoning to a passing waitress, Jayne breathed her request into the girl's ear. Nodding, she slipped into the kitchen.

Some moments later, the girl once again approached their table, bearing a huge, unwieldy tray. Jayne signaled to Bessie, and they began to sing "Happy Birthday." Jayne's strong, lilting voice blended with Bessie's slightly quavery one. On the tray, looking very much like a small bonfire, were thirteen dishes of fried ice cream, each sprouting a single birthday candle.

"How wonderful, Bessie! What a clever idea!"

As Bessie opened her mouth to speak, Jayne shook her head in warning. The reward came from the relief in Bessie's face and the delight in Nora's.

"Thank you so much for asking me to join you!" Jayne beamed down at the white-haired gathering from her loftier vantage point.

"Can't you stay awhile longer, dear?"

"I'd love to, but I do have some things to do when I get home. I have a couple of 'work' problems to think through. Perhaps I can solve them now that I've had such a lovely evening."

Jayne's mind was on Kristin, a young girl who had been missing from her exercise classes for the past week. Jayne felt that she was failing her in some elusive, intangible way. It had been troubling her a great deal, but she had no solution. She needed time to think.

Kissing Bessie good-by on the top of her snowy white head, only Jayne heard her soft words: "Come to church again, Jayne. Have Chad bring you. Please."

Squeezing the little woman's shoulder, Jayne left them, feeling less lonely and more loved than she had in a long, long time.

CHAPTER SEVEN

"KRISTIN IS WAITING outside to see you, Jayne."

Chad stuck his head around the corner of the office door just in time to see Jayne lovingly put one of the small blue birds back onto its perch after a ride on its mistress's finger. She closed the cage door and turned toward him, surprise apparent on her lovely face.

"Kristin? Why, she hasn't been around for days! Is she okay?"

Chad was acutely aware of Jayne's concern for the young and vulnerable girl. Her parents, stymied as to what to do to help the overweight, shy child, had sent her to Jayne on Chad's recommendation. For weeks Kristin had sat quietly in the nutrition classes or moved listlessly in aerobic dance, always three steps behind. Nothing Jayne had said or done seemed to inspire her, and Chad had run out of suggestions as well.

"She looks the same—no smile. But she actually spoke—had to ask for you, I guess. She seems agitated, though. Keeps clasping and unclasping her fingers, like she doesn't know what to do with them. Want her to come in?" Always sensitive to others' feelings, Chad hadn't missed a thing, Jayne thought.

"Please."

Kristin could have been Jayne at age fourteen. Jayne, her own wounds still seeming fresh, ached with the child's misery.

Slipping around the edge of the door at Chad's encouragement, head down, fingers woven together in a vise-like grip, Kristin entered Jayne's office. Even her suffocating shyness could not suppress her curiosity concerning the lovely Jayne Lindstrom's office. Kristin's downcast eyes traveled across the pale peach carpet and followed one desk leg upward toward the jungle-like foliage and twittering birds in the scrolled wicker cage.

"It's as beautiful as you are, Miss Lindstrom!" The words came out in a breathy whisper of amazement before the girl realized what she had done. Then, clamping her lips tightly together, she dropped her head even lower, mortified that she had spoken.

"What a charming thing to say, Kristin! Thank you!" Jayne was eager to put the distressed girl at ease. "Would you like to look at the birds? I just had one out for a moment. Would you like to hold the other?"

Drawing her gently to the cage, Jayne flipped open the door. "Just put your finger in front of him and he'll hop right on."

Nudging her arm upward, Jayne finally got the girl to put out a stubby finger. Immediately the little bird perched on the outstretched digit, bringing to Kristin's face the first smile Jayne had ever seen there.

Sometime later, Kristin regretfully returned the tiny creature to its cage where it dived into the feeder.

Suddenly garrulous, Kristin turned toward Jayne and blurted out, "My mother made me come. She said if I wanted to quit coming to your classes, I had to tell you why."

"I'd like very much to know, Kristin. Is it something I said or did?"

"You, Miss Lindstrom? Oh, no. *You* never do anything wrong. I just feel so out of place. Even ladies my mother's age can do the exercises better than I can!"

Jayne had wondered about that, thinking back to her teen-age years. Berating herself for not understanding sooner, she inquired aloud, "And how about the nutrition classes. Are you uncomfortable there as well?"

"You give me too many choices. Instead of having a half a cup of this and two ounces of that, I just eat lots of everything. What can I do? I hate myself!" Tears welled up in the girl's eyes.

Drawing her close, Jayne hugged her, laying a cheek in the light brown hair long enough to blink back the tears in her own eyes. Recovered, she held the girl at arm's length and announced brightly, "Well, I have some ideas! How would you like to come and work out with me here in my office for a few days—just till you feel comfortable in the group. I'll teach you all the routines. You'll become so proficient that you'll even be able to sub for me if I get called away!"

Jayne watched the watery eyes brighten, interest flickering for the first time. "Really?"

"Absolutely! And for the next part, I need Chad." Sticking her head out the door, she called to him as he came from Buddy's office.

"Chad! Come here! We need you for a moment!" Turning back to Kristin, she grinned conspiratorially and the girl responded, turning a full-fledged smile on Jayne just as Chad came to the door.

Amazed at the change in the girl in only twenty minutes, Chad stared from one to the other, obviously wondering what had transpired between them.

"Kristin and I need your help. *And* the help of your computer. I'd like to feed in all the information and have it come up with a diet for Kristin— in black and white, no choices, no variations. If she follows it, she'll lose one or two pounds a week and be trim in no time. Can it do that?"

"This is a health club; that's what it's for. When do we start?" Obviously delighted at the hopeful look in the girl's eyes, Chad appeared willing to do anything necessary to keep it there.

"I'll give you the information tomorrow. Today Kristin will have to describe her eating habits to me and tell me some of her favorite foods. It's easier to diet if you can eat things you like

75

occasionally." Jayne smiled down at the girl, now bright-eyed with optimism.

"Do you think we can do it, Miss Lindstrom?"

"Jayne. Call me Jayne. Of course we can! I'll even jot down some of the music I use in class and a few stick figures for you to follow. That way you can exercise at home, too." Squeezing Kristin's hands in glee, Jayne allowed a radiant smile to break across her face. The excitement she felt was mirrored in Kristin's face.

Dazzled by Jayne's smile and deeply touched by the loving display of concern, Chad backed breathlessly out of the room, unwilling to disturb the magic of the moment. It was apparent that there was more in this for Jayne than helping one child. There was a catharsis here, allowing her to recapture and finally conquer some of the pain of her youth.

Chad had a difficult time keeping his mind off Jayne's face or his eyes off her office door as he backed down the hallway, deep in thought.

Jayne spotted Chad waiting at the stairwell when she left her office with Kristin. Then she saw his face fall just as she heard Ed hurrying up the hall behind her calling, "Jayne! Jayne!"

Jayne was in a quandary. She knew that Chad had been waiting for her, and she wanted nothing more than some time alone to discuss their triumph with Kristin. Chad, however, seemed to fade from sight whenever Ed came around, unwilling to be a part of whatever troubled web he thought Ed was weaving around her. It was an odd, one-sided rivalry, Jayne mused.

If only Chad would fight back! But he's too much of a gentleman. He'll never make an inconsiderate move, even with Ed around, pushing his way to the fore. A fretful frown flickered across her face. Making a quick decision that, for tonight, she would abandon her scheme and relax in Chad's company, she looked up to tell him so. Her eyes caught only a glint of Chad's gold-tipped head as he slipped down the stairs and out the front door, leaving her once again to the man he thought she loved.

"Jayne! Where should we eat dinner tonight?" Ed's possessive approach was disastrous.

Turning on him with a cold light in her eye, Jayne responded, "I really don't care where you eat dinner tonight, Ed. I have plans of my own."

Leaving him, mouth agape, she went home to a quiet meal in an apartment that seemed far too empty.

"There's quite a game going on in court two this morning, Jayne." Jayne looked up, startled. Buddy rarely talked about the racquetball courts, concerning himself mostly with the weight lifters and the sport shop. Something was up.

"Why do you say that, Bud?" A heavy feeling settled in her stomach.

"Just is."

"Quit it, Buddy! What's going on?" A panicky feeling gripped her. Buddy was acting very strangely.

"You'd better go and see for yourself. Your boyfriend Ed challenged Chad to a game of racquetball. Seemed pretty peeved when he came in. Did you two have a fight last night?"

The truth dawned on her with crystal clarity.
Ed must think I spent last night with Chad!
Now he's trying to prove something to him. Her
mind reeled with the thought.

Hurrying to the spectators' booth, Jayne
looked down on the two men engaged in civilized
combat. Ed was no match for Chad. Though he
had trimmed down and looked 100 percent
improved from his first day at Body Images, he
could never have attained Chad's physical stamina in that period of time.

A light misting of sweat was apparent on
Chad's brow over the red sweatband he wore
around his forehead. The sun-streaked hair was
damp, and the bronze skin gleamed under the
bright lights. Dressed entirely in white, Chad
moved with grace and ease, dancing lightly,
keeping himself loose and centrally positioned to
go after any shot.

Ed's red gym shorts and bright yellow T-shirt
with a smiley-face emblazoned across it were
soaked with perspiration. He was beginning to
swing wildly, not returning shots that, if rested,
he could easily have mastered.

"How long has this been going on?"

"They're into their second hour. Chad wanted
to quit, but Ed wouldn't let him. He's carrying
around some chip on his shoulder today. Told
Chad he wanted to beat him, once and for all."
Buddy laconically related the events leading up
to the challenge match.

"Ed is no match for Chad!"

"You tell him that. Somehow I think this has
something to do with you, Jayne. Ed came in

78

with blood in his eye today, but it looks like the only one he's hurting is himself.''

It was true. Ed looked exhausted; Chad, barely winded, even wearing ankle weights. *Ankle weights!* Chad hadn't even bothered to remove the weights and still he was beating Ed badly. Jayne sucked in her breath in alarm. Ed would be livid when he realized what Chad had done!

Chad was taking shots off the back wall and firing them into corners just above the floor, frustrating all Ed's attempts at victory. He was able to pick a spot and send the ball hurtling to it from almost any angle.

"That's why Chad's the teacher and you're the student, Ed,'' she muttered under her breath. "Are you crazy to challenge him?''

She dodged and swayed with the movements of the two men, living out their fierce battle.

Now Chad was playing the ceiling, sending balls careening crazily off the front wall.

"Chad only has a couple of points until game. Maybe Ed will give up then,'' Buddy speculated, but he didn't believe it would happen any more than Jayne did.

Then Jayne noticed that Ed's breathing was becoming erratic, his face more flushed. She could read Chad's lips, pleading with Ed to quit and rest. Bullish and obstinate, Ed shook his head, picking up the ball to serve.

What happened in the next few moments was obvious to both unseen spectators. Each time Ed served, Chad made a valiant but unsuccessful attempt to return the ball. Some, he kept in play for a moment before seeming to fumble them,

79

losing valuable points. Taking the serve once, he double-faulted, and gave a grand show of disgust at his own carelessness.

When the match was over, Ed was victorious. Chad congratulated him, shook hands, and, in a show of unaccustomed camaraderie, put his arm around Ed's shoulders as they left the court.

Jayne, running to the court door to meet them, saw Chad's arm draped in a friendly manner across Ed's shoulders. His free hand, racquet dangling from the wrist, supported Ed's arm from beneath. He was trying not to show how much Ed was leaning on him.

She read Chad's warning glance and slowed her hasty progress just in time.

"I beat him, Jayne! Not bad for a beginner, eh?" Ed huffed out the words.

"Not bad at all, Ed! You must be a natural at this game." Turning to Chad, she teased, "You'll have to look out for your job!"

Chuckling, Chad reminded her, "As long as I own the business, I get to teach. Remember that when you have to push me in my wheelchair onto the court." Then he turned back to Ed, sincerely congratulating him for the fine game. Then they were lost from sight as they stepped through the swinging locker room doors.

Amazed again by Chad's graciousness, Jayne stood looking at the closed door, wondering what it was in Chad that made it so easy for him to forgive. Ed had tried to make a fool of him. It hadn't worked out that way, but it might have, and Jayne knew Chad would have acted the very same. He'd talked once about "Christian witness." Perhaps this was part of what he had meant.

Jayne wanted to forgive, too, but she couldn't. She still wanted to hurt Ed like he had hurt her. It was an ugly thought, unbecoming and unpleasant. She wished she could learn about forgiveness. Maybe Chad and that church of his could teach her something about it. . . .

CHAPTER EIGHT

"Jayne! I'd like to talk to you." Ed's voice held an unfamiliar urgency.

Jayne pulled in place the cool, disinterested expression that she used with him, and turned to face him.

"Yes, Ed, what is it?"

The more eager he was, the more aloof she appeared to be. It was becoming more and more difficult. When he chose to use it, Ed had a ready wit and natural, easy charm. And his persistence was awesome. Jayne had to give grudging credit for his perseverance in the face of the icy resistance she displayed. More and more she could remember *why* she had once loved him.

"Let's go out tonight, Jayne, for a nice evening—not just coffee at a diner after work. I'd like to make it a really special evening."

She fought the urge to refuse his eager invitation, for it could help to further her plan. What she really wanted was a quiet evening with Chad, laughing and talking over the day's events.

Watching Ed's eager face through half-closed eyes, she used the ploy that had been getting her through these weeks, inspiring her to continue. Jayne conjured up the image of the old Jayne, the heavy, unhappy girl Ed had jilted. Her college days were still fresh enough in her mind that she could nearly smell the antiseptic the janitors used in the hallways, could almost hear the whir of the ventilation fan in her dormitory study room.

She had been intimately acquainted with the low growl of that fan, having spent nearly every evening of her college years studying at a desk below it. She would sit in that study room at her favorite desk, one facing the window overlooking the courtyard below. On more nights than she cared to remember, Jayne watched the couples coming and going into the foyer of the building, often stopping for a leisurely good-night kiss.

She remembered one winter evening in particular. Her biology lab partner had asked her to a concert. Unsure of his motives and afraid of rejection, Jayne had turned him down. And she had sat alone in the study room, watching the couples leave, one after the other, walking through the light, puffy snow that drifted down lazily through the spotlights gleaming from the eaves of the building.

The scene was silent and picturesque, much like the paperweight on her desk. When she shook it, artificial snow showered over a tiny couple in a plastic sleigh. Her life seemed much like those plastic characters on their perpetual sleigh ride—artificial, full of sameness, going nowhere. The only difference—she was going alone.

Some evenings she worked at the dormitory's front desk, but that was more painful still. A steady stream of young men flowed through those doors. From her perch at the desk, she was forced to see the bright eyes and loving touches directed every way but hers. After her shift, she would return to her single room to study, seeking solace in books and her one faithful companion, food.

Jayne pulled herself ten years ahead into the present, her resolve now firm. "Yes, Ed. I'll go out tonight."

He would pay for those years. He had helped to create the lonely, pitiful creature that had been Jayne Lindstrom. He would experience some of the pain of being discarded. But he could not be spurned until he wanted what he could not have. Her goal somehow did not seem as satisfying as she had dreamed it; it was becoming distasteful, sour. Only the image of her past spurred her on.

She felt a twinge of regret as Ed's eyes lighted at her answer. He was delighted that she would go out with him. She remembered when the tables had been turned, and she had experienced that same delight at being asked out by the young Ed Garrett. *Times have changed,* Jayne thought, but something was still missing. Even the thoughts of revenge could not produce the feelings of satisfaction that would make her triumph complete.

"Wonderful, Jayne! I was hoping you would

say yes! I got two tickets to the new play opening at the Guthrie—Shakespeare's *Romeo and Juliet*. Pretty fitting, huh?''

She choked on the bubble of wry laughter in her throat. Their romance was hardly in the class of the classic lovers. Yet—and Jayne pondered the question seriously—was there not a similarity in all tragic love stories?

"I'm sure I'll enjoy it, Ed. I've always been fond of the writings of Shakespeare. Thank you for suggesting it."

"And I made reservations before the play for dinner at that seafood place Buddy is always talking about. Is that all right?" A frown furrowed Ed's forehead. He could, never predict Jayne's moods.

"Lovely. What time should I be ready?"

"I'll pick you up at six. Is that enough time to get ready after work?"

An idea sparked in Jayne's fertile mind. "Plenty. In fact, I think I will just take the rest of the day off. It might be fun to buy a new dress for the occasion. See you at six!"

Jayne strolled off to her office, leaving Ed rubbing his hands together in jubilation. Gathering together her purse and sweater, Jayne hurried out of the club and into her car. She had a lot to do before six o'clock. She had better hurry.

She rushed into the department store, and then came to a grinding halt that nearly set her back on her heels. How could she possibly become transformed in just five short hours? Thinking quickly, she decided that she would start from the inside and work out—one step at a time.

Pausing in front of the lingerie section, her eyes skimmed the display of sheer, frothy apparel. Nothing made her feel more feminine than lovely lingerie. She pulled lacy black garments off the hangers, added a pair of sheer hose, and went to the counter to make her purchases.

Next, she hurried to the designer department. She knew the dress she wanted. She had admired it only last week, but had decided it was too extravagant.

"May I help you, madam?" The clerk's nose appeared to be attached by invisible string to the ceiling. She quivered slightly as she spoke, as if she feared that Jayne might carelessly touch one of her expensive garments.

"Yes. I saw a dress here last week that I'd like to try on. Black, with only one sleeve."

"Ah, yes! I know the one you mean! It was on a mannequin. Am I correct?" The clerk's eyes began to gleam. This was a serious shopper, and the dress was one of the most expensive in the store.

"Yes, it was in that corner." Jayne pointed to a mirrored enclosure displaying a sequined gown.

"Please, come with me."

The clerk led Jayne back through a maze of smaller dressing rooms to a spacious one carpeted in plush rose. Mirrors covered each wall and the scent of incense permeated the room. A large square pedestal about eighteen inches high was centered in front of a massive three-way mirror.

"If you would care to slip off your things, I'll get the dress."

Seconds later she was back, carrying the

86

flowing black fabric across her outstretched arms. She stood on the square at the middle of the room and dropped the dress over Jayne's head and upstretched arms. It flowed silkily down her body until the hem rested in a pool at her feet. Trading places, Jayne stepped up onto the pedestal for a better look and the clerk stepped down to straighten the hem.

It was stunning, there was no doubt about that. Jayne's eyes opened a little wider as she took in the vision before her. It was happening again. She didn't recognize herself.

Her right arm and shoulder were snugly swathed in black fabric which fell away at the collarbone to reveal an expanse of clear, white skin. Her left shoulder was free of confinement as the dress draped under her arm. The dress hugged her body, falling over her slender hips as though it had been designed for her. As she moved, she discovered another interesting aspect of the dress. The skirt was split up the entire left side from hem to the top of her knee, giving a tantalizing glimpse of skin as she walked and postured.

"You have just the figure for that dress, madam—so slender and long-legged. It is absolutely lovely!"

Jayne had forgotten the clerk's presence, so busy was she imagining herself on black, high-heeled slippers.

"Yes, it is nice, isn't it? Do you think it's too long? I need shoes, I believe."

"I will have someone bring shoes up so you can try them on. Your size, please?"

Within the hour Jayne was again on the street, a garment box under one arm and a shoe box containing skimpy black sandals with two-inch heels in the other. Depositing her purchases in the back of her car, she stood with hands on hips, planning her next move.

Thoughtfully fingering tendrils of dark hair, she turned and entered the beauty salon to her left.

"I'd like to have my hair done, please. And a facial and manicure as well."

By 5:45, Jayne was ready. Studying her reflection in the mirror, even she found it hard to believe that less than five hours earlier she had left Body Images in a pair of jeans and a smock. Her hair was now piled upon her head in planned abandon. Tendrils cascaded around her face, giving her kohl-darkened eyes a look of smoky allure. Diamond studs pierced her ears and a single-carat diamond winked from its sturdy gold setting on the chain around her neck.

One long, shapely leg was revealed as the dress fell away at the split, showing a dusky stocking-clad limb and the nearly invisible shoe to their best advantage.

Nervous butterflies flitted through Jayne's stomach. This trickery she was embroiling herself in cast a pall over all she did. Only for a few minutes, when she was having her hair done, had she relaxed and wiped the nasty designs from her mind.

She forced herself to think of the wasted years she had spent trying to regain the shreds of self-confidence that Ed had nearly eradicated. She replayed the chant in her mind, *You're a nice girl, Jayne, but. . . .*

The sound of the doorbell broke her reverie, reminding her that the man about whom she felt so much ambivalence had arrived. She poked the visual button and Ed's face popped onto the screen.

He looked very handsome. His face was slimmer above his dark suit. The early gray at his temples gave him a distinguished air, the black and silver of a bird's wing, poised for flight.

"Come on up, Ed."

Jayne moved slowly toward the door, knowing only Chad could beat her to it from the foyer. She threw open the door just as Ed poised his curled fist to the door to announce his arrival.

He carried a white florist's box in his other hand, balancing the awkward box against one hip. Jayne inspected him from the top of his dark head to the gleam of his lightly polished leather shoes. He had tried very hard this evening. She would have to give him credit for that.

"Here—these are for you." He extended the florist box with a flourish.

"Thank you. How thoughtful!" Jayne opened the box. Cushioned on its bed of tissue was a corsage of red roses, greens and a whisper of baby's breath.

"It's lovely, Ed." And lovely it was, but Jayne again remembered other flowers—a charmingly casual bouquet rather than this intricately constructed affair of blossoms and wire.

"May I put it on for you?" Ed glanced from the corsage, with pin jutting from its stem, to

89

Jayne's one naked shoulder, then to the cloth-covered one.

"Of course. Just be sure you pin it on my left shoulder and not my right!"

Jayne giggled. Perhaps the evening would not have to be dreary after all. After much chuckling over Ed's "all-thumbs" attempts, the roses were secured to their inky background, enhancing Jayne's exotic appearance.

"You're really something, Jayne. I would never have imagined how beautiful you have become." Ed paused to gaze at her, awe-struck. Then gathering his wits about him, he continued, "We'd better get going if we hope to have a leisurely meal and still be at the theater on time."

"I'm ready." *Yes, Ed, I'm really ready for you.* Jayne took Ed's arm as they left the apartment, a confident smile on her carmine lips.

"Ed, there's enough food here to feed an army!" protested Jayne, as they were seated.

Tables of seafood stretched before them. Mounds of steamed shrimp and crab legs rested on beds of ice. Steaming trays of scallops and scrod nestled next to oysters Rockefeller and oysters on the half-shell. A pot of clam chowder bubbled near a vast bowl of lettuce.

"Buddy recommended this place—looks like it was a good choice."

"Ed, have you ever noticed Buddy's size? He won't go anywhere unless he's sure he'll get filled up!"

"I'm busier looking at your size, Jayne. This

will be good for you. If you don't eat more, someday you'll just disappear!"

"Things change, don't they, Ed?"

The question was pointed and Ed winced before he answered. "I deserve some needling about the way I treated you, Jayne. I was wrong and thoughtless and young. Oh, here comes our waitress." It was obvious that this was a subject Ed did not want to discuss.

Jayne did not pursue the matter during dinner. Much to her surprise, she was enjoying Ed's company.

Looking at his watch, he grimaced, and said, "As much as I hate to break up this lovely dinner party, we should leave now so we aren't late for the play. Are you all done?"

"If I ate another crumb, I would break out of this dress!"

"Well, that would attract a crowd and we'd really be late! Come on, let's not keep Bill Shakespeare waiting." Throwing down a wad of bills on top of the check, Ed took Jayne by the arm and steered her to the car.

Shakespeare's spell wove itself around Jayne who even forgot for a magical moment the man sitting next to her and the perverse trickery she had set out to play upon him. The play moved quickly through the five short days of Romeo and Juliet's tragic romance, set against the warring background of their families, the Capulets and the Montagues.

Jayne found herself identifying with the thirteen-year-old Juliet, experiencing her first true love in the faithful and passionate Romeo.

Ed, appearing touched by the impassioned lovers and their untimely deaths, leaned toward her. His breath was warm against her ear as he whispered, "I always wondered where that phrase *star-crossed lovers* came from!"

Jayne's heart lurched in her chest at the words. *Star-crossed lovers*—Chad's face loomed before her. She and Chad were thwarted by circumstance, but it was of her own making. There were no feuding families to keep them apart—only her own taste for reprisal.

Reminding herself of the man who was her escort, she spoke aloud, desperately wishing that a honeyed blond head were in the place of Ed's dark one.

"What a marvelous production! Thank you for getting tickets!" Jayne had been deeply moved by the pathos of the story and the artistry of the players. Unconsciously, she took Ed's arm, alternately squeezing and releasing it in her excitement.

"It is quite a love story, isn't it?" he asked.

"And so tragic! For all of that to happen to those beautiful young people. . . ."

Jayne fell into a melancholy mood as Ed ushered her into his car. Cajoling and teasing, he tried to restore the light-hearted mood of a few moments earlier.

"How about some espresso and a slice of cheesecake?"

"Ed! How can you think of food?" Jayne wrinkled her nose in disinterest. Weakening slightly, she added, "You can have the cheesecake, though a cup of espresso might be nice."

"It's a deal! I found a little hole-in-the-wall that makes espresso, Cappuccino, café au lait—you name it. How about that?"

"Fine. Have you seen much of the city since you've been here, Ed?"

"Some. It's grown a great deal in the past few years. I knew it well when I was at the university. I hate to admit it, but I even got lost on the way to a client's home yesterday!"

Jayne laughed in sympathetic amusement. "That's not surprising! I rarely venture away from my path to work and the shopping malls."

"You must shop somewhere pretty special, Jayne, by the looks of that dress. I was very proud tonight, having the most beautiful woman in the theater on my arm." His voice was low, emotion-filled, with a sincerity that Jayne would have believed impossible.

"Thank you, Ed. That's very nice to hear." She smiled inwardly. The dress was working.

"Here's the place I was talking about." Ed pulled his car into a slot near the front door and tugged the keys from the ignition.

"You're sure they make good espresso?" Jayne was wary of the unobtrusive entrance. It wasn't very promising.

"Yep. Trust me."

Trust you? I've made that mistake before! her brain screamed, but the words were left unspoken, though she shot him a look in the dark that would have set him back on his heels had he seen it. Silently she took his arm and allowed herself to be led into the depths of the building.

Inside, Jayne's eyes quickly grew accustomed

to the dim light. She noted with appreciation the rustic brick decor, with small, private tables nestled under arches and scattered throughout the main room. A lone guitarist sat on a stool at the front of the room, plucking strains of familiar music from his twelve-string guitar. Waiters carried steaming cups on huge trays, holding them high over the customer's heads.

"Well, I'm impressed" she admitted.

"And you'll be surprised by the espresso. Come on, let's sit down." Ed led the way to a quiet table, far from the bistro's other patrons. He ordered for them and then sat staring at Jayne from across the table, a strange, gentle light in his eyes.

"You have no idea how it makes me feel to be here with you tonight, Jayne." He took her hands which she had clasped tightly into a knot. He spread her fingers to their full length, rubbing them gently until they relaxed under his ministrations.

Then he slipped his own hands, palms up, under her outstretched ones until they were resting lightly on top of his.

"Your hands remind me of my mother's, Jayne—long and beautiful. Hers were well-worn, though, by the time I was old enough to notice them."

"Your mother's hands?" This conversation was taking an unusual twist.

"Uh, huh. She had long, shapely fingers like yours. But the nails weren't kept like these." He tapped the top of one lacquered nail with his own clipped one. "She was a cleaning lady. Her nails were chipped and broken. Her hands were chapped from water and harsh soap, but you could tell by their shape that they had once been lovely."

"I never knew much about your family, Ed. I guess I didn't know—about your mother."

"She was the sole provider for me and my younger brother and sister. She worked hard at it, too."

"I remember your younger sister, but I didn't know you had a brother." Jayne was shocked by how little she knew about this man she had once loved.

"Jimmy was the black sheep. He was busy gearing up to get himself sent to reform school about then. I didn't like to talk about it. His antics just about killed Ma."

"I'm so sorry, Ed! What about your father? Where was he when all this was going on?"

She saw Ed's eyes grow moist as he spoke of his father.

"Died when I was eight. Left me and Ma in charge," he said. "I don't think I pulled my share. . ."

"Oh, Ed, how can you say that? You were just a child!" She was surprised to find herself defending him, wanting him to stop blaming himself.

"My mother took on more than she could handle. She cleaned houses all day long and then at night she would clean office buildings. I watched the little kids, but I wasn't very good at it. My brother was bent on trouble from the day he was born. I even did the cooking—can you imagine that?'' He laughed a wry, humorless laugh.

Jayne stared hard at the man before her. He had become a stranger. How could she have known so little about him? Had she been that involved in her own self-pity and insecurity?

"But, Ed, when I met you, you seemed so unconcerned and carefree! And you never acted or dressed as though you had money problems.''

"I was working by then. I started young. In fact, I remember the incident that inspired my getting a job. It was winter. And as you well know, winters in northern Minnesota are cold. Ma had been sick, so she wasn't working. We were never very good about keeping up payments. Everything was hand-to-mouth. Well, we ran out of fuel oil and there was no money to fill the tank. We sat for two days in front of the gas stove trying to keep warm, the oven going, the burners blazing. I'm amazed now that we didn't burn the house down or asphyxiate ourselves by inhaling the fumes!''

Horror spread across Jayne's face. She could imagine the three children and the ill, overworked woman with long, slender hands huddling near that stove.

"I finally went to the fuel oil company and offered to sweep floors, run errands, whatever, if they would give us some fuel. They did. I've been a working man ever since.''

Dumbfounded by his revelations, Jayne stammered, "But, Ed, you seemed so prosperous and sure of yourself! I remember thinking surely your family was rich and successful!'' She could not make his story jibe with the cocksure, arrogant youth who had hurt her so.

"I put on a good act, Jayne. There was no one more insecure than Ed Garrett, and no one who tried harder to hide it. I didn't want anyone to know how vulnerable I was. I'm sure I hurt people with my act. I wonder if you weren't one of them."

She stared at him, jaw slackened. It was as if, in her own home, the doors had been thrown open on a room that she had never seen before. And it was full of both treasures and atrocities. She had misjudged Ed. He was not so very different from herself, after all.

Just when she decided it would be impossible for him to surprise her any further, he pulled a slim foil-wrapped package from his coat pocket.

"I have something for you, Jayne."

"Ed, no. I can't take any gifts from you." She involuntarily backed away from the outstretched parcel.

"Please. It would make me very happy if you did."

It would make him happy. After the sad, emotional story he had just told, she felt an urgent desire to please him. Holding out a trembling hand, she allowed him to place the silver package in her palm. Opening it slowly, with an intensity born of amazement and guilt, she unfolded the wrap to reveal a navy velvet jeweler's box. Inside, on a bed of white velvet, lay a sapphire, suspended from a silver chain, surrounded by tiny, glittering diamonds.

"Oh, Ed, it's lovely, but I couldn't . . . ."

"Why not, Jayne? I want you to have it."

She looked into his eyes. There was no way she could tell him why she did not want his gift, that she would only have to return it later when she sent him to his ultimate punishment. She pushed it away, hating to touch it.

"No. Ed, I won't!"

"Please, Jayne! Think of it as repayment for letting me join Body Images for less than four months. Think of it as all the Christmas cards and gifts I never gave you. Think whatever you will of it, but take it—please!"

He tugged it out of its nest then and unclasped the chain. Standing, he walked around behind her chair and slipped the necklace around her neck. Clasped, the sapphire rested on creamy skin.

"It's not like that rock you're wearing, Jayne, but it's pretty, don't you think?" He was so eager for approval that he nearly wriggled back into his chair, like a small boy.

"It is perhaps the loveliest sapphire I've ever seen. I'll wear it proudly, Ed. Thank you."

The plan was backfiring. Everything was going awry. The last emotions Jayne had expected to feel for Ed Garrett were compassion and affection. But somehow, he was worming his way into the heart she was afraid had turned to stone. Suddenly frantic to escape the strumming guitarist and the intimacy of the secluded table, she pushed her chair backward and stood up.

"Ed, can you take me home now? I'm very tired, and your gift has overwhelmed me." Pale and trembling, Jayne pleaded to leave.

Concern flashed across his face and he jumped from his chair, nearly knocking it over in his haste.

"Are you all right, Jayne?"

Her dark eyes blazed like coals against her white skin. "Just a little tired, Ed. It's been a big day."

Ushering her like a fragile doll from the confines of the bistro into the cool night air, Ed guided Jayne's unsteady steps. Concern written across his brow, he kept one eye on her, the other on the road all the way to HighTower Court.

Jayne lay back against the seat, eyes closed until they arrived at her residence. Turning her head toward Ed as he pulled into the circular drive that spiralled past HighTower's front doors, she smiled.

"Sorry, Ed. I felt faint for a moment, but I'm fine now."

"You scared me, Jayne. I think of you as one tough lady!"

"Not as tough as I thought I was . . . ." The response was a whisper, more to herself than Ed, who had already jumped out of the car and raced to the passenger side. With a gentle hand, he guided her to the door.

"Here's your apartment. This really is a classy place, Jayne!" Ed eyed the plush, long halls and tiny crystal chandeliers that dotted the ceiling in an unwavering row.

Somehow before she knew it, he had maneuvered himself into position, pinning Jayne against the wall. He stood with both palms outstretched, one on either side of her shoulders. She looked up at him, startled, in time to see him lower his dark head to hers, and feel his lips graze hers in a light, tender kiss.

She closed her eyes, not knowing what her next move should be. Taking her mood for acquiescence, Ed kissed her again, less tentatively, taking possession.

Jayne, leaning her full weight now against the wall for support, could feel Ed's lips upon hers but, in her mind's eye, it was Chad's face that reeled before her. She had attained what she sought, only to discover it was not what she wanted at all.

Freeing herself from Ed's embrace, she stumbled into the apartment. Muttering the appropriate words of gratitude, she sent him on his way. Then she kicked off the wispy sandals and padded barefoot to the divan. Crumpling onto its broad expanse, she gave herself up to a flood of tears.

CHAPTER NINE

EVEN THE NORMALLY IMPERTURBABLE Buddy Carlisle glanced at Jayne with concern as she slogged her way into the Body Images coffee room the next morning. Staffers, enjoying a cup of coffee before their daily routines began, looked at each other in wonder. The usually impeccable Ms. Lindstrom looked as if she had not slept a wink the previous night.

Instead of the gleaming blanket of lush dark hair that usually flowed down Jayne's back, rowdy, wayward curls were confined under a red cotton-print scarf. Dark circles pooled under her eyes and rippled out as far as her high, etched cheekbones. Tired and pale, without a dab of make-up, Jayne looked as unlike herself as anyone could ever remember.

She sat down at a small table facing the wall and bent dejectedly over a steaming cup of coffee. One by one, the Body Images staff filed out of the room, until only she and Buddy remained.

"Jayne! Come join me!" Buddy's invitation was more a command. Slow to respond, Jayne risked the threat of him bodily picking her up and carrying her to his table. Reluctantly she pushed her chair back and pulled herself and her coffee cup to where Buddy was sitting.

Just then Chad burst into the room, emitting a charge of electric energy.

"Hi! Great morning! Did anyone see that sunrise? I was jogging and . . ." His voice trailed off at the look Buddy shot his way. Pulling up a chair, he joined his partners around the table.

Chad, too, was appalled by Jayne's disheveled appearance, but said nothing.

"Bad night, Jayne?" Buddy was not so tactful.

"Didn't sleep a wink, actually. I must have dozed off about sixty seconds before the alarm rang. I know I look awful, but I thought I'd get my class plans and reference book and work at home. Maybe I'll be able to nap. Chad, can you ask Wanda to take my classes today? Tell her I'll fill in for her sometime."

"Sure, Jayne, if that's what you want."

"Nice necklace." Buddy had noticed. Jayne's hand flew to her neck. The sapphire and diamond necklace winked under the florescent lights. She should have taken it off, she thought to herself. That was part of the reason she had been awake all night.

The silence of both men spoke more eloquently than words that they knew the source of the expensive bauble. Jayne sensed their surprise, disapproval, hurt.

She wanted to scream that the necklace was only a symbol of ten years' pain, rejection, and misunderstanding. Just as she was preparing to tell her friends the truth, Ed strolled into the coffee room. She saw his eyes go directly to her neck and focus on the glittering jewel. The proud light in his eyes silenced her protest of Chad's and Buddy's disapproving stares.

Knowing now how vulnerable Ed was, Jayne hadn't the heart to let him hear her say that his gift meant nothing to her. She felt a twinge of sympathy for this man and one for herself—one of them would surely suffer. She would not mention the necklace. Buddy and Chad would have to think what they would.

"Did I walk in on an administrative meeting here? Excuse me. I'll grab some coffee and be on my way. I wanted to lift weights and take a shower before I started my business calls today. See you!" Chipper and cheerful, Ed filled his styrofoam cup with steaming black coffee and two scoops of creamer before leaving the room. His buoyancy and confidence contrasted sharply with Jayne's listlessness.

Buddy, arms crossed and eyes darting from Ed's retreating back to Jayne's downcast face to Chad's tense jaw, seemed to be pondering the situation for a moment before he spoke.

"You two missed my announcement this morning."

Jayne and Chad's eyes flew to Buddy's round, impassive face.

"Announcement? What announcement?" Chad's surprise was evident. As business manager, he usually knew everything about the workings of Body Images.

"About the traditional company party."

"What traditional party?" Even Jayne was curious.

"You two newcomers weren't here last year. Every year since I opened the club, I have given a party up at my lake cabin for the staff. This coming Sunday will be the day. Can you come?"

"Well. . . ." Jayne and Chad's voices blended, registering uncertainty.

"Since you and Chad are our newest staff members, you'll be the guests of honor."

"Well, in that case, how can we turn him down? Right, Jayne?"

"I suppose not . . ." Jayne was busy trying to imagine the huge, burly Buddy throwing a party. She had visions of balloons and paper streamers strung through weight machines and piles of dirty socks.

Finally she agreed, "Thank you, Buddy. That's very sweet." Silently she decided it would be worth the trip just to see his cabin, though the prospect of a duplication of his neglected, dingy office caused her to quake.

"Can we bring anything? Food, beverages?"

"Nope. I'll take care of everything. Next year you can help, but this year I'll do the cooking."

Jayne and Chad glanced at each other covertly. It was apparent that both had decided Sunday would be a good day to fast.

"What time do you want us out at the cabin, Bud? And where is it?"

"Come for brunch—any time between eleven and one. I'll give you a map. And stop by for Jayne."

"Is that all right with you, Jayne?" Chad's tone, as he turned toward her, revealed only courtesy. The sapphire around her neck was warning enough not to assume more about their relationship.

"That would be nice. But don't you want to go to church first?"

"I'll pick you up right after the first service. Unless . . . you'd like to go along?" A hopeful look crossed his face.

"Thanks, but I think I'll spend the time getting ready. I'll just be out in front of my building at whatever time you say. Tell me, Buddy, how should we dress?"

"Just bring swimsuits and extra clothing. Someone invariably splits his jeans in a wicked game of volleyball. And it cools off toward evening. The weather report is good for Sunday, though."

Brightened by the prospect of a day at the lake with her friends, Jayne gathered her books and papers together, looking far more cheerful and alert than when she had come in.

"I think I'll go home and do my plans for next week and spend the rest of the day sleeping. If I'm going out for a big day tomorrow, I want to be rested!"

She laid a gentle hand on Chad's clean-shaven cheek, then placed a kiss on the tiny bald spot on

105

the top of Buddy's massive head. Winking at the two, she turned and exited, leaving the men staring at each other across cold cups of coffee.

Jayne was already perched on the brick planter at the front of HighTower Court when Chad arrived. Hoisting a canvas and leather bag to her shoulder she jogged toward the car, her jeans-clad legs churning under the weight of her tote.

"What have you got in there, anyway?" Chad grunted as he tossed the case into the back seat of his car next to his much smaller brown and beige duffle bag.

"Swimsuit, swim wrap, suntan lotion, make-up, change of clothes, shoes, sunglasses, radio and cassette player, tapes, comb, brush, a book, and, just in case Buddy's cooking doesn't work out, a couple of pounds of gorp. That's all."

"That's all? People have traveled around the world with less than that! Entire tribes in Africa don't *own* that much stuff, and you're dragging it all for one day?"

"Sermon was on missions, huh?"

Chad burst into cheerful laughter. "You know me better than I know myself, Jayne. You put your finger on it. And, by the way, what's gorp?"

"Trail mix, like hikers and cross-country ski-ers often take along. It's full of high-energy ingredients like raisins, nuts, chocolate and sometimes coconut. I thought you might like it. It will keep us going through the day if Buddy's cooking lives up to my expectations! If Buddy is more of a cook than I suspect he is, he can put it in his candy dishes. That is, if he *has* candy dishes!"

Jayne's voice trailed off at the specter of Buddy's dishes. She could see a vast table set with the tops of coffee cans for plates, mayonnaise jars as glasses and an array of mismatched utensils, including pocketknives, for silverware.

"You're a little apprehensive about Buddy's entertaining capabilities too, huh?"

"More than a little. I can't imagine his cooking anything more than those horrible raw egg concoctions he whizzes up in the blender at Body Images."

"Well, I've found that Buddy is a man of many talents. We may be pleasantly surprised." *Leave it to Chad—the eternal optimist!* she thought.

Jayne studied her traveling companion as he drove. Chad guided the car with one hand, his left elbow propped on the open window ledge. Wind whipped through his golden hair, blowing it back off his face. Framed by the window, every curve and angle of that face was profiled against the blue sky. The collar of his red and white striped shirt stood up rakishly at the back, ruffling the golden strands at his hairline. His foot tapped impatiently at the accelerator, the muscles of his leg moving under the crisp white pants.

Tearing her eyes from the disconcerting view, she glanced out toward the countryside. Now that they had left the city behind, trees were becoming more plentiful on the rolling hills.

"You look nice today," Chad smiled at the lovely girl on the seat beside him.

"Have you had breakfast?"

"No, I haven't. I meant to, but getting ready took longer than I had anticipated."

"I didn't eat, either. Maybe we ought to break out some of that goop you brought along, after all. Somehow I don't feel like going to Buddy's on an empty stomach—"

"It's *gorp*!" she corrected, laughing delightedly and reaching into her bag to produce the package. They nibbled from the mixture as they rode in companionable silence.

"This can't be right!" Chad's voice broke through Jayne's semi-conscious state induced by the rhythm of the car and the warm sunlight streaming through the window.

"What? What's wrong?" Jayne bolted upright in the seat, thinking something was amiss.

"Buddy gave me very specific directions to his cabin, but this can't be right!"

They were parked at the end of a long, woodsy lane. Overhanging trees created a leafy tunnel leading to a huge, rustic A-frame house.

"Well, we can walk up and ask directions. Do you think Buddy's cabin is just a trailer parked on the lake, or something?"

"He didn't say, but this is hardly a lakeside cottage. I doubt this would be his place."

Just then Buddy appeared on the deck, wearing a chef's apron and waving a pancake turner.

"Hey, you two! Up here! Walk up and come on in—I'm cooking!" With that he turned and waltzed back inside.

Chad and Jayne stared at each other, agape,

then pulled their bags out of the back of the car and started for the house, Chad lugging Jayne's huge pack while she carried his lighter one. They walked through the tunnel of trees, staring from side to side in sheer amazement. Whatever they had expected, it certainly wasn't this—this mansion.

As they neared the lovely A-frame, they noticed the plush green lawn angling down to a sandy beach. A well-kept dock where a flashy orange and white speedboat was moored fanned out over the water. Flower gardens flanked either side of the narrowing path. Near the side of the house was a bricked patio containing a huge gas grill. A clothesline full of wet swimsuits dried in the sun that filtered through the trees surrounding the house.

Buddy met them on the deck as they approached the house. Now they could read the black letters on his syrup-splattered apron: "I'm Not A Good Cook. I'm A Great One!" He waved the pancake turner their direction and invited them inside.

"Come on in! There are plenty of pancakes and sausages left. Everyone else decided to arrive early and have a swim before brunch."

Open-mouthed, Chad and Jayne walked into the cabin, taking in everything with wide eyes. The narrow galley kitchen admitted only Buddy, wielding his spatula. There was room for no one else between the cluttered counters and steaming electric frying pans.

Body Images employees were everywhere. Some were just finishing their meal at the trestle table near the kitchen. Others were sipping coffee from steaming mugs and lounging on the massive pine furniture scattered about the room. Nick and Carla were reading the Sunday paper. All were complaining about being too full, and giving Buddy rave reviews as cook.

One entire end of the living area was glass, overlooking the plush carpet of lawn and the crystal blue lake. In one corner a spiral staircase wound its way to the loft above—an open area which served as Buddy's bedroom. Jayne could see the foot of a king-sized bed covered with a homemade quilt jutting toward the rails that enclosed the loft.

Music blared with a syncopated beat throughout the cabin. On the tables Buddy had even placed arrangements of fresh flowers from his gardens.

Jayne and Chad stared at each other in mute astonishment.

Jayne found her voice first. "Buddy, we never dreamed you had a place like this. It's so . . . *unlike* you!" Then she cringed at the implication of her words.

Buddy only grinned in understanding. "That's what everyone says, but there's a reason." Reading the curiosity in his friends' eyes, he continued. "Mary, my wife, and I bought this place when we were first married. We built it from nothing. She loved to garden and I liked to hammer and saw. We had some wonderful times working here together. And after we had our little boy, they got even better. After they were both killed, I couldn't bear to give the place up.

There are all sorts of happy memories here. Mary liked it groomed and polished, so that's how I keep it. I like it that way too, even though you'd never be able to tell it from the looks of my office." Buddy's smile had turned tremulous.

"This is a lovely tribute to your family, Bud." Jayne felt tears scratching at the corners of her eyes. Each time she thought she understood someone, a new and shining facet appeared to surprise her.

Chad, recovering from this unexpected revelation, rubbed his hands together. "Well, let's taste this gourmet cuisine I keep hearing about."

"How many pancakes do you want?" asked Buddy. "Four? Five? I've got five on the griddle."

"Four is plenty. We had—uh—a little snack on the way," Chad confessed. "Where's the sausage?" He went snooping under frying pan lids until he discovered what he wanted. Spearing several tender links, he settled himself at the trestle table.

"How about you, Jayne? How many pancakes?"

From the impish expression in Buddy's eyes, Jayne knew she was being teased. "One small one, please."

Everyone in the room groaned, having consumed a minimum of four each. It was no wonder Jayne stayed slim as a reed.

"Buddy, this is a side of you I never dreamed existed!" Chad shook his head in wonderment as he devoured the last of his pancakes.

Chuckling, Buddy responded. "I'm full of

surprises, old boy. Someday you may find out a few more!''

"Good, but for right now, I'm tempted to try out those lawn chairs in the sun. Want to come along, Jayne?''

Jayne took the hand Chad extended and they strolled onto the deck and settled themselves in the lounge chairs mounded with colored pillows.

It was a lazy, glorious day. Later, Chad and Jayne swam in the crystal clear water, able to see the sandy bottom and an occasional minnow darting below. For what seemed an eternity, they lay immobile on the inflatable rafts, drifting this way and that with the undulating water.

Their peaceful interlude was broken by a call to a vigorous game of volleyball and then more swimming to cool overheated bodies. The hours drifted by and both were amazed to hear Buddy clanging a rusty Chinese gong by the front door and yelling, "Supper time! Come and get it!''

"Didn't we just eat brunch?'' Jayne asked suspiciously, wondering how the day had been telescoped into only a few minutes.

"Yup. About six or seven hours ago. Would you rather eat gorp?'' They laughed together over their private joke.

But the joke was on them when they spied the two-inch thick steaks sizzling on the grill and dozens of baked potatoes, cut open and filled with golden pats of butter. A mound of sour cream stood sentry.

"Help yourself. There's corn on the cob in the big metal cooker—grew it myself, so no complaints. Rats! I almost forgot the fruit bowl!''

112

Buddy threw down the mitted potholder he was wearing and dashed into the cabin. He returned bearing a huge hollowed-out watermelon, filled with a wealth of strawberries, blueberries, cantaloupe and watermelon balls, nectarines, pineapple, and kiwi.

Finding a secluded place near the crowd, Jayne and Chad sat down with their heaping plates.

"Chad, this pineapple is the sweetest I've tasted in ages!"

"I didn't get any. Let me taste."

Jayne held out a piece of pineapple. Instead of taking it from her, he leaned near and bit into its woody sweetness, his lips closing down around her fingers. Startled by her reaction to the gentle pressure of his lips on her fingertips, Jayne quickly withdrew her hand and picked up her fork. But electricity sparked between them, as bright and visible as the fireflies beginning to flit now in the gathering dusk.

"Hey, you two! You'd better get over here if you want to see your cake!" Buddy bellowed from the picnic table on the patio.

"Cake? We'd better check this out." Grabbing Jayne's hand, Chad pulled her up from her seat and they walked arm and arm toward the rest of the group. In the center of the wooden table was a huge, rectangular cake, marked with the serving lines of a racquetball court and inscribed in bold chocolate letters: "Welcome to Body Images, Jayne and Chad!"

"That's wonderful, Buddy! Don't tell me you decorate cakes, too!" Jayne touched a corner of the frosting with a tentative finger.

113

"Not yet. But maybe by next year. I ordered this from the bakery."

"Well, it's beautiful. And does it represent all those double faults Chad's been making lately?" Jayne teased lightly, having picked up on Chad's racquetball woes.

'No fair!" Chad wailed. "For that, you have to cut the cake!"

"Right. And here are the plates." Buddy shoved a stack of plates and a serrated knife in Jayne's direction.

Laughing and talking, the threesome served the cake to their employees. Soon only crumbs were left where the confectionary court had once been—except for one piece Jayne had saved for Chad. With more symbolism than she realized, she laughingly held the moist cake to his lips—newlywed fashion. Catching her wrist, Chad pulled her to him, his eyes locking with hers for a spellbinding moment.

CHAPTER TEN

THE HUM OF MOTORCYCLES biking the trails around the lake marred the late afternoon, droning like pesky mosquitoes in the stillness. Jayne watched Buddy's face darken. The buzz of those low-slung, bright-colored three-wheeled cycles had been flitting in and out of her consciousness all day. If they were irritating to her, what must Buddy be feeling? Though radically different from the huge Harley-Davidson cycle Buddy and his wife and child had been riding the night of their accident, these little motorized tractor-like machines could be nothing but a reminder of that tragedy so many years ago.

Jayne lazily watched Buddy from her comfortable nest beside Chad on the patio. She saw him visibly shake off the melancholy mood and pick up the rectangular cake pan, spearing crumbs with one large forefinger.

The buzz of the three-wheelers was edging

closer, and two bright orange cycles with oversized black wheels spun around in the sand at the foot of the slope fringing Buddy's lot.

Buddy drew in a sharp breath, muttering something unintelligible under his breath. Then, he spoke again, more loudly this time, "Fools! Don't they know how dangerous that is?" His knuckles tightened around the cake pan and Jayne could see it buckling under the fierce pressure he was exerting.

Carla and Nick, two of the club's oldest employees, walked with studied nonchalance toward their employer. Jayne, from her neutral perch, could see others moving in as well. Without wanting Buddy to realize it, they were rallying around him, trying to deflect the memories that haunted him.

"Where are you taking that pan, Carlisle? I still see some cake there. Did you have plans to go inside and polish off the pile of crumbs all by yourself?" Nick sauntered toward Buddy.

"Yeah! I suppose you thought you'd get the last of the coffee too!" Wanda chimed in.

"Coffee! That reminds me, Buddy. I brought a whole pound of freshly ground Black Forest chocolate! Let's brew a new pot and throw out that dishwater you made." Carla teased him more boldly now, as the somber expression faded from his face.

"Dishwater! I make better coffee than the whole lot of you put together. I should fire you all and start over!"

"Hear! Hear! The man thinks he can replace us!" Everyone burst into peals of laughter. Jayne

116

and Chad sat watching the scene, arms wrapped around their knees, grinning from ear to ear. The din increased as Buddy took more playful ribbing, and the disquieting moment passed. No one noticed the three-wheelers and their riders spinning and turning, insinuating their way toward Buddy's private dock.

Suddenly, a scream split the air. Before the scream had died away, a dull, bone-jarring thud and the sharp snapping of metal and hard plastic could be heard. Jayne's eyes flew to the beach where one of the three-wheelers was disabled— the seat, buried in the sand; three fat, black wheels upturned, spinning madly. Next to the dock lay a crumpled rag-doll figure, limbs splayed brokenly on the sand. A rivulet of blood had begun to meander a course down the man's cheek.

A whimper brought Jayne's attention back to the patio. She could not believe her eyes! In place of the strong, laughing giant of a moment before was a small, frail shell of a man. It was as if the essence of Buddy had been torn from him at the sound of the screams and torn metal, leaving a pitiful remnant still clutching the dirtied cake pan.

Chad, frozen for a moment, now catapulted into action.

"Nick, Carla! Get Buddy inside! Wanda, call an ambulance! Hurry!" Chad's legs churned toward the dock, passing the others who were making their way toward the gruesome scene.

No one questioned Chad's authority as he fired instructions.

117

"A couple of you take care of the other rider. He looks pretty shaken up, but I don't think he's hurt. From what I could see, this guy ran into one of the braces under the dock and caught one wheel. Don't touch him!" Chad nearly screeched the command as someone bent over the prone figure. Jayne caught up with them just in time to hear his explanation.

"It could be his back or his neck. If we moved him just a fraction, we could be doing terrible harm."

"But, look at that leg, Chad, the bone is completely broken off. It's . . ."

"I know, I know. Never mind that now," Chad chided gently.

Hot bile rose in Jayne's throat as she looked at the broken bone protruding through the man's pants' leg and the blood that streaked the already blackening side of his face. Only Chad seemed oblivious to the sickening sight. He was moving as close to the wounded man as he could, talking softly.

Chad turned back to those standing behind him. "Someone had better go watch for the ambulance just in case Wanda was too rattled to give good directions. And bring down some blankets. Light-weight ones if you can find them. We should keep him warm until help comes."

"Can I do anything, Chad?" Jayne whispered so softly she was afraid he wouldn't hear.

"Stay with me, Jayne. Tell the others to help Buddy. He needs his friends right now and I . . . I need you."

Following Chad's instructions, Jayne sent the

others back to Buddy. Taking the blankets Wanda had dragged from the house, she brought them to Chad who was kneeling next to the young man's head, talking soothingly and running gentle fingers over his brow and through blood-matted hair. Jayne could barely hear what Chad was saying, so close was his mouth to the prone man's ear.

"It's going to be all right. The ambulance is on its way. You'll be fine. Don't try to move. I'm going to put a blanket over you. I won't touch you. I'm right here, right here . . ."

Chad stood to cover the man, wiping his blood-stained hands on his pants. He seemed oblivious to the horrible sight, speaking as if he and the conscious but silent man on the beach were old and dear friends.

Why isn't he repelled by all of this? Jayne could hardly bear to keep her eyes on the bloodied, agonized face before her, while Chad was only inches away, talking softly, cheerfully. She shuddered and shut her eyes for a moment. When she opened them again, Chad was still kneeling near the man, his own eyes closed.

"Chad, what are you doing? Chad, are you okay?"

The green eyes opened and Jayne could see gentle amusement in them. "I'm praying."

"You're *what*?"

"*Praying!* I think the situation calls for prayer, don't you, Jayne?"

"Well, I suppose so . . ." she stammered.

"Try it. He needs all the prayers he can get."

Jayne clamped her eyes shut in an imitation of

119

Chad, but realized with astounding and disturbing clarity; *I don't know how to pray!* Whatever Chad did when he prayed was beyond her, but instinctively she sent up a sincere petition to the God Chad was so sure was listening, *Oh, help! Please help!*

"The ambulance is here, Jayne, they're bringing the equipment down the hill."

Her eyes flew open. White-clad men were making their way toward the pitiful little cluster on the beach. Chad stood and ran to meet them to explain what had happened. Jayne turned her back on them as they prepared the man to be moved. She could not bear to hear the piercing moans emanating from the stretcher area.

When she turned again, the stretcher-bearers were plowing through the sand and up the slope toward the house and the flashing red light at the top of the hill. Chad was moving slowly, alongside the litter.

It was as Jayne caught up with the procession that she realized the injured man was clinging to Chad's hand so tightly that his fingertips had darkened slightly with the pressure. Chad was still chanting his comforting litany.

"It's going to be fine. You're in good hands now. They'll take care of you. It's going to be fine . . . ."

Chad pried his hand loose from the convulsive grip as they slipped the litter into the open doors of the ambulance. The doors shut on the prone figure, and the driver turned toward Chad.

"Thanks for not trying to move him. Smartest thing you could have done. Might have made a difference between his walking again and being permanently paralyzed. We'll have the hospital give you a call later.''

Chad nodded briefly and stood in the driveway watching the receding taillights until they were lost to view. He turned then and embraced Jayne tightly, as if drawing strength from her presence. Suddenly Chad straightened.

''Buddy! I've got to talk to Buddy!'' Chad grabbed Jayne by the hand and pulled her toward the A-frame. Inside, the others sat or stood helplessly by. Buddy was nowhere in sight.

''Where is he?'' Chad demanded.

Nick nodded toward the darkened loft. ''He says he doesn't want anyone up there, Chad. He's just crushed. This brought everything back. He keeps repeating his wife's and child's names over and over.''

''He'll talk to Jayne and me.''

''No, Chad. I can't interfere in this. I know so little about it,'' Jayne protested.

''It's not interference, Jayne. It's love. Buddy has helped both of us through some tough times. Now it's our turn. Come on.''

They mounted the stairs with cat-like tread, but before they reached the top a ragged, tear-filled voice met them.

''Go away.''

''Sorry, Bud. Not now. We're coming up.''

''Chad?''

''And Jayne. Turn on a light.''

''Go away.''

''No. Turn on the light before we stumble.'' Jayne was amazed at Chad's calm persistence.

121

Unoffended by Buddy's words, he gingerly felt his way to a bedside lamp and flicked it on, putting Buddy in sharp relief.

Blinking wildly at the bright light, Buddy ran a hand across his reddened eyes.

"You don't listen very well, do you?"

"No. Neither do you. Are you okay, pal?" Chad sat down on the bed next to his friend and threw an arm across his bent shoulders.

"I will be. It just all came back to me . . . Mary . . . and the boy . . ." Buddy's shoulders shuddered with a sob.

Simply and with such love as Jayne had never witnessed before, Chad embraced his friend. Jayne, touched by the scene, struggled for breath against the tears and swell of emotion she felt welling in her throat.

So this is how people can love each other!

She stood, spellbound. She could virtually see Buddy's sagging shoulders rise and square under Chad's warm ministrations.

What kind of man is this, anyway? Chad was deeper, more complex, more wonderful than she had imagined. Listening intently, she heard him speaking softly, urgently.

"I've been through it, Bud. I know how it feels. For months after Timmy drowned, I woke up in a cold sweat, thinking I was swimming, that I could save him this time. And I never could, Bud. He kept sinking out of sight and I couldn't reach him . . . . It's been nearly twenty years since my brother drowned, and I still remember. But you remember the good times more."

"Look at this house, Buddy. It's just like you

122

and Mary planned it. You said so when we arrived. Hold on to the happy times, Bud. You're going to have lots more of them."

A voice from the first floor broke into their conversation. "Hospital just called. That fellow is going to be fine. Several broken bones and a concussion. He's conscious and said to tell the guy that stayed with him 'Thanks.' "

Chad slapped Buddy across the shoulders and grinned a quirky, irresistible grin.

"See, things are improving already. Even though it's been a long time since you lost Mary, you remember how much you loved her. Just like I loved my brother. It's okay to remember. It's worse to forget."

"How did you get so smart, twerp?" Some of the old zest had returned to Buddy's voice.

"I was wondering that myself. How did *both* of you get so smart?" Jayne stepped up to the two men, loving them more than ever before.

"I didn't know I was all that smart, but I did wind up with you two as partners. That must have been a flash of pure, unadulterated genius!" Buddy muttered.

Jayne threw her arms around the burly giant on the bed. "Buddy, you old teddy bear, I love you!"

Chad stamped a foot, just missing her bare one.

"I'm being the nice guy, and who gets hugged? This irascible old bear! No fair! Just for that, Buddy, you're going to have to go down and cheer everyone else up by yourself. Let 'em know they've been wasting their time worrying about you. Jayne and I will stay up here, and she can apologize to me properly!"

"No you don't, Richards. I'm not leaving the beauty and the beast together in *my* loft!" Buddy grabbed Chad by the arm and prodded him toward the staircase.

Chad turned back to Jayne, his finest comedic expression in place, and parried, "I'd be mad at him for saying that if I were you, Jayne. I know I'm a beauty, but you'd *hardly* qualify as a beast!"

Jayne grinned as Buddy maneuvered the wise-cracking Chad down the stairs, the bomb now defused, the crisis over. Suddenly serious, she stared at the golden head from the top of the stairs in bemused wonderment. Chad had depths of strength and wisdom beyond understanding. Her heart thrilled at the sight of him. Her mind reeled with his name. *Chad . . . Chad . . . Chad.*

On the first floor, the guests were starting to gather their things together, preparing to leave. Wanda and Nick were silently cleaning the kitchen. Most were milling about, unsure of their next move. Buddy solved the dilemma with a shout.

"Where does everybody think they're going, anyway? This party isn't over! If you went home every time something went awry at Body Images, we'd be out of business! Let's end this evening on a happy note."

Murmurs of assent swelled in the room. Chad turned to Jayne who had slipped down the stairs behind him, and, laying a caressing palm on her cheek, he said, "How about a sunset swim before we go?"

Nodding her agreement, she picked up her tote. As if on cue, those preparing to leave settled into chairs or meandered back onto the deck and patio area. If the bosses weren't leaving yet, neither were they.

The sun was setting at the western end of the lake, silhouetting the pines against the red-gold circle of fire, when Chad and Jayne, clad in swimsuits, walked into the blaze of color and headed for the water.

Romping on the soft, pale sand, they played like children, running toward the water until it lapped at their toes, then turning and retreating from the icy licking.

In a bold move, Chad took a running dive into the water, sliding head-first into its depths. Those at the cabin could hear him call, "Come on in, Jayne! The water feels good once you get used to it!"

Soon her slim figure joined his, and they splashed and swam until the sun threatened to dip behind the horizon. Walking out of the water together, with the final glorious blaze of sunset burning behind them, they made a striking picture walking toward the beach house. Two perfect bodies —the golden glow of sunset on their skin, flecks of fire illuminating Chad's gold hair, veins of flame like burning embers on Jayne's dark head.

With a sharp intake of breath, someone on the

deck spoke softly: "They look like they belong on the front of a greeting card, don't they?"

Nodding in the near darkness, Buddy added more to himself than to the others: "The perfect image . . ." Then he let out a bellow. "Hey, you guys! We need you up here!" Buddy was standing on the deck swinging a guitar over his head. "We need somebody who can play this thing!"

Chad groaned, "Don't tell me the guests of honor have to perform!"

"Well, I certainly hope *I* don't!" Jayne echoed. "I've never even held a guitar!"

"You're the lady vocalist, then. Let's go. Maybe if we're good enough, we can take this show on the road." Chad jumped up and pulled Jayne along with him. Shrugging into terry cloth jackets that Buddy tossed their way, they slipped into a gap in the circle of people gathered around the outdoor fireplace. Buddy was handing out wire coat hangers and bags of marshmallows.

Sitting cross-legged near the fire, Chad took the guitar from Buddy's outstretched hand. "Let me have that thing before you wreck it, Carlisle."

"It's all yours, Richards. Literally. I stole it out of your office last night."

"I thought it looked familiar."

Strumming the strings lightly, Chad played some tentative chords, humming softly to himself. Warmed up, he looked around the group. "Well, what do you want to sing first?"

Flooded with requests, he skillfully complied, his fingers flying over the frets, his rich, full voice leading the others in song.

126

Soon they were singing gospel hymns. Buddy's deep bass voice resonated, welling up from deep within his chest, mingling with Chad's, rich in harmony. Jayne felt tears prickle at the back of her lids. It had been a lovely day, joyous and peaceful. She would treasure it forever, no matter what happened in the future. Chad. Ed. *Chad.* . . .

Reluctantly, the party was breaking up.

"I suppose the bosses will be mad if we're all tired tomorrow."

"Yeah. Especially if the bosses are tired tomorrow, too!"

"Gee, I hate to leave without helping with dishes, but you know how it is . . . ."

"Thanks for everything. It was a super day!"

The voices and laughter trailed away as the guests gathered their belongings and headed for their cars. Soon only Buddy, Chad, and Jayne were left.

Having slipped into a white jumpsuit, Jayne returned to the main room where Chad and Buddy were having a final cup of coffee. She came across the room toward them, and stepping over Chad's long legs, leaned over to give Buddy a hug.

"Buddy, you absolutely amaze me! Thank you for a lovely day."

"Thank you for coming. Maybe next time I invite you for dinner, you'll trust me."

Jayne shot Chad an accusing glare. "You told him, didn't you!"

Hurt and innocent-looking, Chad waved a hand in front of his face. "I just told him that we were

127

having a little trouble imagining him as a cook and housekeeper. And he put us in our places royally."

"Well, he can invite us again anytime. But we'd better get going right now. It will be late enough by the time we get home."

Chad set his coffee mug down on the pine coffee table and stood up, stretching himself out to his full height and rolling his shoulders back. "I'm about ready to fall asleep now. Jayne will have to keep me awake all the way home."

Laughing, they left the house and climbed into the sleek sports car. Jayne leaned her head back against the head rest and settled herself for the ride. Chad turned the key in the ignition and the car glided onto the road.

With her eyes closed, Jayne could have guessed whose car this was. Chad's scent was everywhere, tangy and masculine. Not only his scent, but his sound. Bright, cheerful gospel music spun from the interior speakers.

Experiencing an unusual, if somewhat tenuous feeling of peace, Jayne lay back to savor the feeling of Chad's caring for her, bringing her safely home. He was quiet now, humming along with the melody of a song, but not speaking. Occasionally he would glance over at her and give her a warm, cockeyed smile.

Too soon he pulled up in front of the HighTower building. Switching off the ignition, Chad turned his body toward Jayne, resting his right arm over the back of the seat, his hand burrowing in the wave of hair flowing over the back. The

128

blue-white street light played on the angles of his face.

Unsmiling, he studied Jayne's upturned countenance. Neither seemed to breathe. Slowly, almost imperceptibly, Chad's face came nearer, until she could feel his warm breath across her cheek. His green eyes appeared deep emerald in the faint light before his lips came down over hers, capturing her willing ones.

Responding to the slow, gentle kiss, Jayne surged up in her seat and threw her arms around Chad's neck, entwining her fingers in the golden tendrils at its base, pulling him against her in a harder, more passionate embrace. Time hung suspended.

Chad's voice, raspy with emotion, broke the spell. "Jayne. Oh, Jayne . . . ."

Her dark eyes flew open, exposing the white on all sides of the dark irises. Frightened by her response, she fumbled for the car door. Releasing the handle, she pushed the door open with one foot and slid out behind it before Chad's outstretched hand could stop her.

"Chad, I don't know . . . I can't . . . I must go."

Like a timid doe, startled by the hunter, Jayne turned and ran into the night.

CHAPTER ELEVEN

JAYNE SUFFERED THROUGH another tormented night. Wheeling through her brain until the first light of dawn cracked the sky were the faces of Chad Richards and Ed Garrett. Bewildered and confused, Jayne knew that she could no longer hold herself aloof from either man. Both had made inroads on her emotions—Ed on her sympathy; Chad, her passion—and something less tangible. Berating herself for her dilemma, Jayne struggled to sort through her tumultuous feelings.

The cool, indifferent Jayne Lindstrom would never have allowed this to happen. Somehow, in some way, she had changed, become a person she did not recognize. She had lost her vindictiveness, her icy hauteur, her detachment. She was vulnerable again, like the plain and heavy girl she despised from her youth.

Perversely, she had begun to like the man she

had once hated, and to love another who would never tolerate the ugly scheme she had conceived. She would lose them both! Jayne desperately needed time to think.

Slipping quietly into the front door at Body Images, she was grateful that the hallway to her office was empty. More fortuitous yet was the mail she discovered on her desk. A bold, brightly colored brochure invited Ms. Jayne Lindstrom to attend a diet and nutrition seminar in San Francisco.

Glancing at the date, Jayne was surprised to discover the seminar was less than a week away. Relatively unconcerned with incoming mail, she rarely checked the box, trusting Chad to put anything of interest on her desk. He must have held this with the other mailings until there were enough to bother taking to her office. She would have to hurry if she were to make arrangements to attend.

Unwilling to admit that she was running away, Jayne busily called airports and hotels, relieved when the last of her plans was settled. She was committed. No one—not Chad nor Ed nor Buddy—would be able to dissuade her. She could escape, postpone the inevitable confrontations with both the men in her life, and she could sort out what she must say to them and how best to say it.

She sought out Buddy and Chad in the coffee room, wishing to tell them of her plans under conditions in which she could not be questioned too thoroughly.

"Jayne! Hi! We thought you'd overslept!"

131

Buddy looked as rested as ever. There were no telltale signs that he had cleaned his cabin until well after midnight and then driven back into the city.

Even more clear-eyed was Chad, dressed in chocolate brown and ivory, sipping a glass of orange juice and eating a cheese Danish.

A wavering smile appeared fleetingly on her face. "No. Up with the birds. I wanted you to be the first to know my plans."

Chad cocked one eyebrow inquisitively, surprise apparent on his face.

"I've made arrangements to go to San Francisco to a seminar. I'll be needing a week off. Two days' travel time, three days there, and at least one day to get ready. Will that be a problem?" Jayne knew what an integral part of Body Images she was. Of course it would be a problem, but Buddy and Chad would never concern her with the details.

"Well, Wanda and Carla can help out. We'll make do. Have you been thinking about this long?" Buddy's eyes narrowed slightly as he questioned her.

"No. The brochure was on my desk this morning. I've needed some of the information they are offering there, and I thought it would be a good chance to brush up. Since I left the hospital, my work has changed drastically. This should keep me fresh and up-to-date." It sounded very logical, Jayne thought. Chad's raised eyebrow was her only signal that he doubted her story.

Just then, Ed burst through the coffee room

door, whistling cheerfully. "Hi, everybody! What's new?" He poured a cup of coffee and plunked down by Buddy.

"Jayne's leaving for San Francisco." Buddy dropped the bomb, fuse lighted.

"San Francisco? What's in San Francisco? When?"

"I'll be attending a seminar, Ed. Nothing spectacular."

"Does it have to be right now?" His meaning was plain. He didn't want her to leave just when their relationship seemed about to blossom.

"I'm afraid so. You men will just have to struggle along without me for a week or so."

"We'll try to have the building intact when you return." Chad was smiling slightly. He appeared least concerned of all that she was leaving. A pang shot through her.

Buddy caught her in the hall as she left the coffee room. "What's this all about, Jayne? I didn't know you were so crazy about seminars."

She winced under the pressure Buddy was exerting on her upper arm. "I need time to think, Buddy. My life has gotten overly complicated and a little out-of-hand lately."

"Who is it? Ed or Chad?"

She laughed wildly. "Both! Neither! I don't know! Please, Bud, cover for me. I need time to think." Her dark eyes pleaded with the impassive mountain beside her.

"Okay. Come back with some ideas for new programs if you can, and some sourdough bread and chocolate bars if you want to stay on my good side!"

133

"Thanks, Buddy. I won't forget." Jayne gave him a grateful smile and hurried down the hall to her office. She had a lot of loose ends to tie up.

Leaving the building two hours later, Jayne passed by the weight room. Much to her surprise, Ed and Buddy were working out on the machines, chatting and puffing, sweat dripping off both faces. Amazed by the display of friendliness, Jayne refrained from making her presence known. She wanted to keep her life simple. Buddy and Ed visiting companionably after their weeks-long battle was far from simple.

As she was about to leave the building, she remembered her briefcase, still lying on one of the blue love seats where she had tossed it. Returning to her office to retrieve it, she passed by the spectator windows on the racquetball courts.

Chad and a lovely, fresh-faced young woman were playing. Or at least Chad was attempting to play between bouts of laughter. It was obvious that the girl, a novice, was enjoying the attention of her handsome instructor. She held out her hand, racquet facing the forward wall, displaying a weak and ineffective grip. Chad came around behind her and, stretching out his arm next to hers, corrected the grip, speaking into her ear.

The intimate scene sent a pang of remorse through Jayne, sharp and jagged, like a bolt of lightning. Feeling more alone than ever, she hurried away from the cozy scene before her. *Everyone has someone*, she thought bitterly to herself. *Everyone but me*.

And deep in her heart, she knew she had put

herself in this position, isolated, remote. She had carried the bitter seed of revenge too long. Now it was bearing fruit, and the fruit was distasteful. It would drive Chad away when he learned of the secret she had been harboring. And he would soon find a girl, much like the pretty one on the court. Chad would not be alone for long. Loneliness seemed rather to be Jayne's destiny.

The airport was bustling. A handy skycap relieved her of her bags and she checked through her gate. Sinking down in a molded plastic chair near the door through which she would depart, she shut her eyes, closing out the cheerful bustle around her.

"Jayne! Jayne Lindstrom! Is that you?"

Groaning inwardly, Jayne opened her eyes to a mere slit to see who was paging her.

Elizabeth Nelson, an old college friend, was tramping toward her, lugging a bulging, bulky carry-on bag.

"How are you, Jayne? Going to San Francisco, too? I was hoping I'd run into someone I knew!" Liz beamed down at the inert Jayne, delighted with her find.

"Hello, Liz. Long time, no see."

"I'll say it is! How have you been? You look wonderful!"

"Fine. And you? Don't tell me you're living here now!"

"No, just changing planes. You *are* going to the seminar, aren't you?"

Nodding slightly, Jayne replied, "Uh huh. I

don't know what I'll pick up, but I needed a change of pace."

"Aren't you at University Hospital any longer?"

"No. I left nearly a year ago. I'm part owner of a health club now. I'm in charge of diet programs, nutrition seminars, exercise classes, and the like. It's a related field, of course, but certainly different from hospital life."

"That's how you got so skinny and gorgeous! I'd sign up for anything if I thought it would make me look like you!" Liz fondly patted a slight roll hanging over her skirt. "Where are you staying?"

"At the hotel where the seminar is being held. On Union Square."

"Me, too! Maybe we can do some sightseeing together!"

"Maybe." Jayne had not counted on this intrusion. She needed desperately to be alone to think. But perhaps the ebullient Liz would be good for her, preventing her from sinking into the doldrums she felt coming on.

"Flight 729 to San Francisco is now loading at Gate 3." Jayne could barely make out the garbled message over the intercom.

"Come on, let's go!" Liz shot up like a jack-in-the-box, pulling her travel bag behind her.

Eyeing her friend's unwieldy luggage, Jayne was thankful that all she had to concern herself with was the slim, navy envelope purse and navy felt fedora she would put on once she reached the city.

Boarding the plane, she sank gratefully into a

window seat just over the wing. Liz battled with the bulky carry-on until she had wrestled it under the seat. Giving it one final, vicious kick, she satisfied herself that it was secure and tumbled into the seat next to Jayne.

"How can you be so calm, cool, and collected? Whatever you've done to yourself over the past few years should be bottled and sold. You'd make a mint." Before Jayne could respond, Liz pulled a pack of chewing gum out of her pocket and popped three pieces into her mouth. Chewing vigorously, she explained. "My ears and my nerves can't take this up and down business. I close my eyes and chew until we're up in the air. If I'm still at it when breakfast arrives, poke me."

Jayne smiled at her violently masticating friend and closed her eyes, enjoying the powerful rumblings of the plane beneath and around her.

"Breakfast, madam?"

Startled, Jayne's eyes flew open. She had fallen asleep for a few moments and the stewardess was leaning over her, breakfast tray in hand. Liz was grinding away on her gum, eyes squeezed tight.

"Yes, I suppose so . . . ." She looked hesitantly at the foil- and paper-wrapped parcels before her.

"Liz, you can come up for air now. Breakfast is served."

"Whew! If I had had time, I would have taken the train! But then I wouldn't have met you!"

"Or had a chance to eat this meal." Both women stared at the strange concoction Jayne had uncovered on her plate. A large, greasy sausage and pale scrambled egg shared the divided plastic dish with canned pineapple and a garnishing cherry.

"Ugh!" Even Liz didn't like the looks of the sausage. Heartburn was written all over its casing.

Both picked at their food, promising themselves tender croissants and mounds of fresh seafood as soon as they arrived. Laughing and chatting about events in the years since they had parted, the time passed. Soon they were searching through moving lines of luggage for their own baggage.

"Share a cab to the hotel?" Liz looked hopeful and reminiscent of a beast of burden under all her luggage.

"Sure. How long before our first meeting?"

Flagging a cab with her one free finger, Liz responded, "There is one lecture tonight at seven. The schedule I received promised that it would be over by nine-thirty, so we could go out for dinner then. Chinatown?"

Jayne breathed a sigh of relief when she finally closed her hotel room door behind the short, talkative bellboy who helped her to her room. Since Liz was tied up with convention details, Jayne had nearly five hours to do as she pleased. She glanced hopefully at the message light on her phone, but it was unlit. Chad and Body Images were functioning without her. Even Ed had not tried to reach her.

Sighing, she picked up her bag, tilted the

fedora to a jaunty angle, and headed out into the brisk Frisco air. The cable cars were a must. Under renovation the last time she was in the city, they were something she didn't want to miss. She could ride the cars to Fisherman's Wharf and be back in time for her meeting.

Walking swiftly to a point where she could catch a car, her heels rapped a sharp staccato beat on the pavement. She felt very much alive here. Invigorated.

As a cable car clanged to a halt, she fought the crowd to step aboard. Feeling fortunate to find a seat on the rapidly filling trolley, she looked down the first steep hill toward the bay. Holding her breath as the brakeman released the brakes, the car jerked to life and began barrelling to the sea.

Stepping off at the end of the ride, Jayne could see the big sign welcoming visitors to Fisherman's Wharf. Tourists milled about, shopping in sidewalk stands, snapping pictures. It came to her then that perhaps she was overdressed in her crisply elegant suit.

Dismissing the thought, she wandered among the stands, savoring the strong fishy odors. Suddenly hungry, she eyed the vendors selling fresh seafood from beds of ice. She bought lunch of fresh shrimp served in a clear plastic cup with a tiny plastic fork and headed for the water. Settling on the weathered wood, she ate the tiny shrimp one by one, relishing each morsel as she watched the massive freighters plowing through the water.

Sated, she began her aimless wanderings again,

pausing to watch a mime juggling imaginary balls in the crisp sea air. Peeking into a tiny closet of a shop, she found on sale bags of sea shells in delicate hues of pink and peach. Impulsively she purchased a bag. They would be lovely in Chad's aquarium among the waving fronds of seaweed.

Strains of guitar music floated her way. A young, bearded man sat in the midst of a gathering crowd, creating amazing tunes on a shabby guitar. A battered hat was at his feet and an occasional passer-by would toss a coin within its rim.

Fascinated, Jayne stood to one side listening. He played like Chad, his long slender fingers wrapping themselves around the neck of the instrument with nimble ease. Strumming with his thumb and picking out notes with the fingers of his right hand, he began playing some of the gospel tunes Chad had plucked out of his guitar at the lake cabin.

Suddenly desperately lonely, Jayne turned and stumbled away from the scene, tears welling in her eyes. Pulling herself back into her guise of carefree tourist, she racked her brain for the next site on her agenda.

Alcatraz. Everyone who came to San Francisco must surely see Alcatraz.

Staring out over the water at the island shrouded in mist, Jayne began to ponder her own personal prison. She nearly laughed aloud at the irony of it all. She was her own jailer, restraining herself from life, living on its fringes, afraid to love.

The evening lecturer droned on and on. Bored and sleepy, Jayne and Liz eyed each other surreptitiously. Soon a note came drifting Jayne's way from Liz's outstretched hand.

"I'm starved! Do we dare leave?"

Nodding, Jayne slipped out of the hard metal folding chair and into the aisle. Immediately businesslike she strode from the room as if on a vital errand. Liz, imitating the purposeful walk, followed her into the hall.

"Gee, you do that well!"

"Do what?" Jayne cast a startled glance at her friend.

"Walk out of a meeting like you really had somewhere important to go! And I just followed in your wake!"

"Well, I do have somewhere important to go— Chinatown. All the talk made me crave chicken almond ding!" Laughing, Jayne and Liz made their way to the cab stand at the front of the hotel.

Disembarking in the midst of another world, the two stood for a moment, sensing the lure of the Far East. Vendors were out in the streets hawking their wares. Ornate dishes, colored fans, and woven baskets glimmered in the street lights. Cubbyhole shops were open for business, many displaying gaudy tunics, straw slippers and silk pajamas.

Impulsively Jayne stepped into a tiny shop to admire a scarlet silk robe displayed on the back wall. A gold and green fire-breathing dragon coiled around the body of the garment, its scaly green tail curling itself across the scarlet expanse

141

of the back. A savage snout appeared to disappear around the other lapel. Only the eyes were benevolent, benign. They glowed green and kind.

"What a wonderful robe!"

"The one with a dragon on it? Somehow I can't imagine you in that, Jayne."

"Look at the dragon's eyes! He's all fierce and flaming, but his eyes are gentle. Just goes to show that the exterior doesn't tell the whole tale!"

"Well, I've spent my entire budget already on tea sets and fans. You should have *some* souvenir of our evening in Chinatown."

Much later, laden with packages, the two women made their way into a tiny restaurant. Relaxing over the sumptuous meal of won tons, egg rolls, fried rice, and chicken almond ding, they began to reminisce. While sipping tea from a tiny handleless cup, Liz began a gentle inquisition.

"Tell me about yourself, Jayne. Any men in your life? Or maybe that's a dumb question to ask someone so beautiful!"

Jayne's eyes grew suddenly remote and misty. She was remembering Chad strumming the guitar, firelight flickering on his golden hair. They hardened, then saddened slightly as she recalled Ed. She looked across the table at her friend. "Men? There are some—too many, I think, or maybe not enough. It's a long story, Liz. You don't want to hear it."

It was obvious that Liz *did* want to hear the tale, but Jayne was not willing to share it. Her turmoil over Chad and Ed was too painful, too private.

"Why don't we head back to the hotel? We have a full day tomorrow."

Liz nodded in agreement, yawning. "I'm flying out right after the conference closes. How about you?"

"I'm not leaving until the next morning. I thought I'd spend an extra evening here." She left the rest of her sentence unspoken: *To think about Chad and Ed.*

After fond good-bys to her friend who was once again dragging the bulging bag to the airport, Jayne set her mind on gifts for her friends. Buddy was easy; it was Chad who seemed impossible to buy for. Having prowled through all the posh department stores in the heart of the city, Jayne decided to try some more trendy locales, like the recently renovated Pier 39 and Ghirardelli Square. If Buddy requested chocolate, she knew he would expect them from there.

A shopping bag full of chocolate and the famous San Francisco sourdough bread later, Jayne emerged from the cluster of shops housed in the old Ghirardelli chocolate factory. Buddy's shopping was done. She had even purchased something for Ed. She could not erase the revelations of their last evening together. She had misjudged the man, and in doing so, had sent her own life on a perverse, unproductive path. The least she could do before she told him the truth was present him with a peace offering of sorts.

In the depths of her bag was a miniature pewter racquetball player, arm stretched high overhead in a vain attempt to return some invisible pewter ball. It would please him that she thought of him that way now, athletic and strong. Perhaps he would throw it away when she told him of her scheme, but at least she would have tried to express the friendship that had blossomed in the most arid and unlikely of all places, her heart.

All of Pier 39 did not seem to contain the right gift for Chad. Browsing through shop after shop, Jayne hardly noticed the darkening sky or threatening clouds. Just when she had decided to give up, she found the perfect gift. In a jewelry case, amidst golden baubles and fine ornaments, was a hammered silver cross on a thick silver chain. The cross rested on a bed of burgundy velvet in a fine rectangular case.

Not counting the cost, Jayne pointed eagerly to the cross. She could already picture it at Chad's neck, resting just below the point at which his collarbone joined and near the spot at which the fine golden mat of hair on his chest began.

"That one, please. In the burgundy case."

"You have excellent taste, miss. That was done by a local craftsman. We have it here on consignment." The elderly clerk handled the box with loving care.

"Can you wrap it, please? It's a gift."

"And a lovely one, too. It's a fine and lucky friend who will receive this." Chattering on, the frail old elf behind the counter prepared Jayne's

144

package, never realizing that his words had sent her spinning off into the pit of regret and despair she had been avoiding all day.

A fine and lucky friend .... Chad was hardly lucky. Jayne's stomach churned at the thought of his disappointment when he discovered the truth about her. Open, guileless, frank, he would never comprehend the reason for the web of deceit and vengeance she had spun for herself and Ed.

On the flight home, Jayne reflected over the past few days. Her moments of introspection had only confirmed what she had begun to suspect— that the insecurity-ridden Jayne Lindstrom was her own creation!

She had spent ten years blaming Ed Garrett for her woes. Only now, when it was too late, did she realize where the real blame lay. She had conquered her body—only to discover that her problem resided in her own mind and spirit.

This time away had proved only one thing— that she loved Chad far more than she realized. Dear, good, honest Chad. But along with that realization came the knowledge that she was unable to give up her stranglehold on Ed, too deeply committed to withdraw now without an explanation. Ed would be hurt no matter what she did. The damage was already done. She would have to see her plan through to its bitter conclusion.

Jayne sighed. She had made a journey—but as was typical of her life—she had gone nowhere.

CHAPTER TWELVE

THE RACE HAD BEEN WON, but the victory was hollow. Jayne's vindictive scheme had succeeded beyond her wildest expectations. Ed was head-over-heels in love. Showering her with gifts and accolades, he spent hours planning surprises that would please her, make her smile. And Jayne was smiling a good deal less than he would have liked.

Miserable and guilt-ridden, Jayne hated every thoughtful gift, every lovely flower—not because they came from Ed, but because soon she would have to tell him what a terrible thing she had done, toying with his affections, not loving him at all. He was as enamored of her as she had once been of him—hanging on her every word, waiting for some crumb of affection to fall.

"Jaynie, how could I have missed seeing before how lovely you are?" Ed was seated on the arm of a loveseat, swinging one leg and looking like he almost belonged now at Body Images.

Looking up from the files on her desk, Jayne smiled cooly, "I'm the same person you knew ten years ago, Ed, only there's considerably less of me now. We both know that's what made the difference."

She ran her long fingers upward through her hair, leaning her head back into the massaging fingers. She'd been having headaches lately, and this routine seemed to help. Her inky hair flowed through her wide-spread fingers like strands of silk, dropping like a waterfall onto her neck as the fingers reached the crown of her head.

Her scarlet velour running suit reflected the scant color of her otherwise pale cheeks. *Funny,* she thought to herself, looking at Ed through half-closed eyes, *all my life I've tried to lose weight. Now I can't eat and the pounds just slide away.*

Standing, she walked over to the open window, letting the warming sun stream over her, so slim she barely made an obstruction in the view of the city.

I've got to tell him. I can't go on living a lie. But wouldn't you know, I've learned to like him! The agitated thought raced through her brain.

Things had not gone according to plan. She didn't love Ed, but neither did she have that burning desire to hurt him. She'd come to understand his bluster and cock-sureness. It was only a cover for the frightened man inside. He'd no more meant to hurt her so many years ago than she desired to hurt him now. She knew now that Ed had only needed a pretty girl on his arm to bolster his confidence. Had he been more sure of himself, more aware that looks didn't matter, none of this would have happened.

And I've lost Chad as well, she groaned silently.

Dragging one finger across the finely veined leaf of a plant, following its age-old pattern, Jayne thought of the pretty young girl who had begun coming to Body Images with Chad several days a week.

From her sweetness and the trusting air about her, Jayne suspected that she was from his church. The girl greeted Jayne with the same warmth Bessie Norheim had demonstrated so many weeks ago, and she was fond of Chad— that was more than obvious. It would be difficult not to love Chad. He seemed to be getting more beautiful himself as the weeks wore on.

He spends an awful lot of time working out, Jayne thought. She would see Chad, both day and night, lifting weights, drilling difficult shots on a empty court, running. He had the look of a finely tuned race horse ready for a win. His gold-tipped hair had grown longer, curling slightly at the base of his neck, giving him a youthful, rakish air. Only his eyes hadn't improved. They were dark and sad, restless-looking.

But there had been a smile in them this morning when he brought Julie Swenson in to play handball. She wondered more than idly how Julie was doing with her first lesson.

Aloud, she said to Ed, who was now lounging

in a wicker chair, "I'm going to see how the handball lesson is coming. I'll see you later."

Nodding agreeably, Ed responded, "Nice girl Chad found for himself. They'll make a good pair."

Turning sharply to hide the look of sudden grief on her face, she went into the hall and hurried toward the courts. Body Images was looking particularly impressive these days. The thought gave her the only pleasure she had recently enjoyed. Cleaning crews had been steam-cleaning carpets, polishing the light oak woodwork, and buffing grayed-glass light fixtures.

Now the plush burgundy carpets in the lounge areas appeared fluffy and new. The sturdy gray carpets in the heavy traffic areas were fresh and clean.

Jayne eyed the pale gray wallpaper with its bright burgundy geometric shapes. She was pleased with the combination—contemporary yet functional. The windows were all treated with louvered blinds, the same burgundy as the plush carpets.

Peeking into one of the lounges on her way down the hall, she smiled at the sight. She had personally chosen the gray pottery vases that graced low-slung wooden tables, and had arranged the dried flowers, baby's breath and burgundy pompoms. Silver framed prints and posters hung low on the walls for easy viewing at eye-level from the reddish-blue couches.

Body Images bespoke the quiet, rugged elegance and good taste that she had envisioned. It was a healthy, healing haven for those who came here. Acoustical tiles muted the noises from the courts and Jayne could hear strains of Prokofiev's "Peter and the Wolf" coming over the sound system. She smiled ironically at the sound. Some days she simply didn't know if she were predator or prey.

Jayne met her quarry coming out of the court, damp and laughing. Chad mopped Julie's brow with the fleecy white towel strung around his neck.

Jayne pasted on an artificial smile and inquired brightly, "Well, how was it, Julie? Do you like handball better than racquetball?"

"Whew! I haven't decided. Chad says you're good at this, Jayne. I don't know how you do it! You look so small to be so athletic!" Admiration glowed in the younger girl's face.

Why can't she be unpleasant? I'd rather be able to hate her! Jayne thought to herself.

Aloud, she responded, unable to resist Julie's innocent charm, "I had a good teacher. If you stick with Chad, you'll be good at it, too!"

The brown-haired girl turned a bright, well-scrubbed face to Chad's, "Do you think she's right? Do you think I'll ever learn?"

"Jayne's never wrong," he answered the ebullient Julie. "Even the most unlikely prospects turn out great, if she says so. Remember Kristin, the little gal who goes to our church?"

"The one who's started singing in the choir?"

"Yep. A few weeks ago you couldn't have gotten her up there for anything. Now she's chirping like a songbird, thanks to Jayne's boosts of confidence." Chad glanced at Jayne with respect. Everyone knew that she had worked miracles for that girl. But today she looked as if she needed some for herself.

"Is something wrong? Troubles with Ed?" he asked, perceptive as ever.

Oh, Chad. Don't ask. Don't remind me. Knowing that Chad had found Julie, Jayne was unwilling to confide in him anymore. She loved him enough to let him go.

"Don't worry about me, Chad. Ed and I will be just fine. You two run along and have fun."

"In fact, Chad," Julie's voice was pitched high with excitement, "why don't you come home for supper with me? Mom made pounds and pounds of Swedish meatballs this morning. She was peeling potatoes when I left. I know how much you love meatballs and mashed potatoes."

"Corn? Was she going to make corn, too?" Chad questioned her hungrily.

"Well, if we get there and put in a request, I'm sure she will. There's plenty of time. Even if she doesn't have corn, will apple pie do?"

"Apple pie! Well, why didn't you say so sooner? Let's go! See you later, Jayne." He put one finger out and chucked Jayne under the chin with a brotherly smile.

Squeezing his wrist just a trifle longer than necessary, Jayne then turned from him and hurried down the hall, blinking back the tears that threatened to fall. Julie and Chad had an easy, familiar camaraderie that she envied mightily. Julie was eager, fresh, and open, so unlike Jayne, whose shyness and insecurity often made her appear cool and haughty.

Envying Julie's sunny charm, Jayne pondered the girl's relationship with Chad. They blended so well as a couple, yet rarely, to Jayne's relief, did they touch. Then she laughed wryly at herself. "What do I know of what they do in private? Chad is too much of a gentleman to make a public display. . . . " She remembered his passionate kiss. Putting a finger to her lips, she could almost feel it there still—arousing, tantalizing, wonderful. But she would not stand in Julie's way. Julie was more what Chad deserved—honest and good, and those were the very characteristics Jayne felt she lacked. Head hanging dejectedly, Jayne made her way down the long corridor.

Thump.

She bolted smack dab into Buddy's wide barrel chest, nearly knocking the wind out of herself, yet barely jarring the burly mountain before her.

Finally there was an excuse, however trivial, for tears. They flowed in rivulets from her dark eyes, down her cheeks, through the carefully applied make-up, and into the gentle, calloused hands that cupped her chin.

Leading the sobbing, hiccuping girl into his office, Buddy frantically looked around for a place to put her. Jayne, in the throes of a full-blown cry, stood sobbing and gulping, unable to stop.

Pulling the olive drab blanket from the cot and spreading it across the vinyl press bench, Buddy ensconced her there and went looking frantically for a box of tissues. Finding them crunched under several days' mail, he waved them under her nose. Finally, he tugged several out of the box and thrust them into her upturned palm.

Breathing in gulps, Jayne finally began to pull herself together. The sight of the hulking giant hovering over her, helplessly gripping a mangled tissue box, struck her funny bone and, through the tears, she began to laugh. Sounding at first more like sobs than chuckles, she choked out the sounds, building behind themselves until a genuine hearty laugh bubbled out.

Chuckling himself, Buddy plunked down on the bench beside her, flung a beefy arm around her shoulders and held her tightly, laughing with her until they were both exhausted.

Sitting with her tousled head nestled on Buddy's expansive shoulder, Jayne turned her tear-streaked face up to his. His broad face was only inches from hers; the pale blue eyes, full of mute compassion. Sandy hair curling untidily around his ears and comical sweetness on his huge features made him look very much like a bigger-than-life teddy bear—someone she could talk to, confide in.

"Oh, Buddy, what am I doing to do?"

"First, you'd better tell me what you're talking about. I think I could hazard a guess, but maybe I'm wrong."

"Chad. Ed. What else?"

"I thought so. It's been like working in a pressure cooker these past weeks."

"I thought I was keeping my feelings to myself." Jayne sat up, alarmed that she had been so transparent.

"Don't worry—you have. I meant Ed and Chad. Those two have been like a powder keg and a match meeting each other in the halls. It's a good thing that Chad's such a gentleman, or we'd have had a blow-up already. He's been keeping the lid on things around here for weeks."

"He is a dear, isn't he?" Jayne's tremulous smile wavered and her eyes filled with tears. "I wish I'd realized just how special he was before. Now, it's too late."

"Too late? Too late for what?" A look of puzzlement crossed Buddy's face, and a frown furrowed down the bridge of his nose.

"Too late for Chad and me. Too late for me to avoid hurting Ed. And now that Julie is involved, too late not to hurt the innocent bystander if I speak up. I've woven a web of deceit that a spider would be proud of, Buddy. I've strung Ed along all these weeks, priming him for a fall. He hurt me badly once, and I wanted to do the same to him. But you know what happened along the way? I learned to like Ed, to understand him. Now I don't feel like hurting him and I have to."

"I don't get it, Jayne. Why hurt him now if you've changed your mind?" Buddy struggled to put the pieces of this confusing jigsaw in place.

"I can't stop. The wheels are already in motion. Ed's fallen in love with me—and you know I can't return his affection. It's Chad I love, but I've chased him away . . . right into Julie's arms. I've seen them together every day since I returned from San Francisco!"

"Well, I don't think Julie. . ."

"Loves Chad? Of course she does! How could

154

she help it? I've never known anyone more lovable! And, anyway, she's right for him.''

"And exactly what is that supposed to mean?" Buddy crossed his arms, looking disbelieving—a burly guru pondering this new information.

"She goes to that church of his. She thinks like he does. My family never attended church. I'd never fit in. I don't think I have ever fit in *anywhere*." The tears came in torrents now, flooding her cheeks.

Buddy folded her in a comforting embrace and held her until she sobbed herself into a deep and dreamless sleep. Gently, once he was sure she wouldn't waken, he carried her to the saggy cot and laid her down, covering her with the olive throw. He left the room, turning back only to switch off the light, a thoughtful, pleased gleam in his eye.

Waking several hours later, Jayne struggled up from the deep valley of the cot and swung her legs over the side to the floor. Standing, she tested her balance. Every fiber of her body ached and felt out of synchronization, like she'd been battered in a fall. Eyes scratchy and mouth dry, she searched the room for a mint or a pitcher of water. Spartan as Buddy lived, there were no such luxuries available. Reluctant to be seen in the coffee room until she pulled herself together, she wondered what she could do to rinse the tears from the back of her parched throat.

Chad's office! The power-packed protein punch. His tiny kitchen. Slipping unseen out Buddy's door and into Chad's, she made her way

155

through the dark, empty office to the kitchen. Flipping on a recessed light, she found the small refrigerator. Squatting near the floor, she peered into its recesses, delighted to see a treasure trove of canned juices and fresh fruits.

Suddenly ravenous after the cathartic cry, she pulled two cans of unsweetened orange juice and a cluster of grapes from the metal grid shelves. Standing with hands full, she tapped the door shut with her foot and took her booty to the coffee table.

Guzzling down one can of juice and popping the grapes, one by one into her mouth, Jayne felt a sudden surge of energy as the natural sugars hit her bloodstream. Sipping from the second can more leisurely, she picked up the tattered Bible that Chad always left lying on the chrome and glass affair.

Flipping through its pages, Jayne was amazed to find words, sentences, entire paragraphs underlined, starred, and notated in Chad's clear, bold script. Not a page was unmarked. Everywhere Chad had found things he thought important enough to mark. Jayne began reading.

The Bible had fallen open to the gospel of Matthew, and as Jayne skimmed the lines, a verse leapt out at her, marked in red ink, stunning her with its simple yet profound message.

> You have heard that it was said, 'An eye for an eye and a tooth for a tooth.' But I say to you, Do not resist one who is evil, But if any one strikes you on the right cheek, turn to

him the other also, . . . I say to you, Love
your enemies and pray for those who perse-
cute you. (Matt. 5:38-39; 44 RSV)

Here it was. Here was the wisdom that would
have kept her out of all this trouble. Turn the
other cheek. Demanding retribution for Ed's
immature behavior had hurt no one more than
herself. The dawning realization of what she had
done, the magnitude of her error all but overwhelmed her. She was suffering, Ed would
suffer, and Chad . . . what about Chad?

Thumbing through the pages, she came upon
another passage, marked in red, the page sprouting a scrap of Body Images note paper as a
bookmark. It began to dawn on her that these
red-marked passages were recent. Perhaps Chad
had come here for guidance as well. Her thoughts
were confirmed as she read the lines.

'Lord, how often shall my brother sin
against me, and I forgive him? As many as
seven times?' Jesus said to him, 'I do not
say to you seven times, but seventy times
seven.' (Matt. 18:21-22 RSV)

Chad was suffering, too, struggling in his own
private battle. How he must have sacrificed to be
generous to her and Ed, enmeshed in their sick
little game! How often had Chad had to forgive
them for hurting him? How often had Chad
turned the other cheek? Chad had come here, to
this tattered volume, to find strength to cope with
her inconsiderate, unpredictable actions and
Ed's insufferably pompous airs.

157

Sick with remorse and shame, Jayne slunk out of the office. She hurried down the long corridors, on wary lookout for the late-night cleaning crew. Tears fell again as she slipped into the little silver car. Arms folded across the wheel, she rested her head on her forearm. Salty droplets fell for some time onto the scarlet legs of her sweatsuit before she pulled herself together enough to turn the key in the ignition and start for home.

CHAPTER THIRTEEN

WHETHER BECAUSE OF HER DEEP SLUMBER in Buddy's office or the whirling demon thoughts in her mind, Jayne could not rest. Tossing and turning on the pale green sheets, even the silkiness of the fine percale could not soothe her. The bed would not yield to her restless churnings, and there was no position in which she could find comfort.

Like the proverbial drowning victim, she relived her life in laboriously slow motion, seeing it pan before her, unfolding the events that had culminated in this sad and frustrating state.

Like it was yesterday, she could visualize a plump, sad-eyed reflection peering back from the mirror in her mother's bedroom. Only eight, Jayne could remember the taunt she hated most, "Plain Jayne, plain Jayne: Can't fit on a train!"

Tossing wildly to rid herself of the pitiful vision, another took its place, slipping into her memory, unbidden. *Eighteen years old. Unstylish. Lonely. Ed.*

Cocky, darkly attractive, popular Ed was the first man ever to pay attention to the withdrawn Jayne Lindstrom. She could see him yet, grinning crookedly, stealing her heart . . . and tossing it aside.

She had isolated herself then, throwing every ounce of energy into her classwork. Jayne Lindstrom—summa cum laude graduate of her college—chief dietitian for University Hospital—still as miserable, obese, and alone as ever.

Then Jayne had discovered the newly opened health club and Buddy Carlisle, and her life began to change. The workouts were her lifeline to sanity. With Buddy's support and friendship encouraging her to continue her regimen, she had blossomed. The weight slipped away, the muscles responded, the years of studying fashion magazines paid off.

Grinning slightly, she remembered the day Buddy had approached her about becoming a partner in Body Images.

"You've become one gorgeous woman, Jayne, and I'd like to see it happen for others. I've been thinking that if I took in two more partners I could expand, add classes. That's where you'd come in. With your background, you could teach nutrition classes, lead diet groups, and teach the aerobics and stretching classes as well. I've got another fellow lined up who's a whiz at business administration and racquetball. With that combination, I'll have my bases covered."

Chad. Dear, consistent Chad. How could she

ever have thought of him as a playboy? But she had. She'd kept him at arm's length too long, afraid that he was just another man who would toy with her affections . . . like Ed.

An eye for an eye. That was no maxim to live by, but she had, for ten long years. Only now did she know that she had been missing something, something that Chad had discovered long ago. *Turn the other cheek. Forgive not seven times, but seventy times seven.* These thoughts rolled through her brain all night until the early morning sky lightened, and the sun cracked the night with its glowing intensity.

Exhausted but still unable to rest, Jayne dropped her legs over the side of the bed, wiggling her toes into the deep, furry carpet. Using both hands to hoist herself to a standing position, she plodded toward the mint tiled bath, and made her way to the shower, turning it on full force. In an uncharacteristically careless gesture, she dropped her nightgown to the floor and stepped under the pelting bullets of water. As the steam rose around her, she savored the almost painful sensation.

Some time later, her hair once again dry and groomed, Jayne sat in front of the expanse of vanity that ran the full length of the bathroom. Dabbing on concealer and thick creams, she attempted to mend the ravages of the night before.

"It's no use! I look just like I spent a sleepless night, bawling my eyes out! No product made can hide that!"

Talking to herself, she began to slap lids back

161

onto jars and brush swabs and cotton balls into the wastebasket beside her. "Haggard! That's how I look, haggard!"

Shrugging her shoulders, she stood, tipping the vanity stool over behind her. Turning to look over her shoulder at the offending stool, she wrinkled her nose, then stepped daintily over it, leaving it upturned. Somehow it didn't matter today if her home was topsy-turvy. It simply mirrored the turmoil within. Somehow, nothing seemed to matter . . . .

Restless and full of nervous energy, Jayne decided to take a walk. Pulling a plum shirtwaist dress over her dark tresses, she fastened a single gold chain around her neck. Then slipping stocking-clad feet into a pair of plum suede low-heeled pumps, she grabbed a tiny suede clutch for keys and cash and left the apartment, escaping the smothering silence.

Once on the street, she remembered it was Sunday, for the normal sounds of congested traffic were missing. In their place was the more leisurely pace of Sunday drivers. Unaware of her ultimate destination, Jayne found herself standing in front of the little gray chapel she and Chad had attended.

The wooden double doors were flung wide, but few were entering. Glancing at her watch, she realized that services did not start for nearly half an hour yet.

Perhaps I can slip in unnoticed. The thought surprised her. She hadn't planned to come here, and now she was considering going inside.

Unaccountably drawn, she followed her instincts and slipped through the welcoming doors before she had a chance to turn and run.

The organist, shuffling through her music, was the only person there. Jayne slipped up the stairs to the balcony and into the farthest row, nearly invisible behind a supporting pillar.

The organist glanced her way, then turned her attention to the instrument, flipping switches and adjusting lights in preparation for the service.

Shortly others began to arrive. From her bird's-eye view, Jayne could see some familiar faces from her last visit. Interested, she sat up, leaning forward to study the crowd. Her heart lurched within her and her pulse began to race as she recognized the sun-streaked head belonging to Chad. He was walking down the aisle toward the front of the sanctuary.

He was alone, dressed in an off-white linen suit cut in the slim, European fashion that fairly radiated elegance. The pale green shirt and deeper hued tie made his hair seem more golden than ever.

He smiled a greeting to an elderly couple sitting near the front of the church and slipped in beside them, settling himself in the pew. He reached forward to get a song book, one gold-tipped forelock falling into his eyes. His broad shoulders shrugged as he relaxed into place and Jayne noticed the hair falling appealingly over his shirt collar.

He's not taking good care of himself. He needs a haircut, she thought idly. The thought was bittersweet, Jayne dearly wishing she had the right to run her fingers through that enticing silk and remind him. But she had forfeited that privilege. Instead, she had pushed them eons apart, foregoing all her rights to a man like Chad.

Julie came into the sanctuary soon after, surrounded by what appeared to be her family. *She has lots of brothers*, Jayne thought to herself as Julie settled herself between the four hulking young men in a pew. Her father took one end of the long bench and her mother, the other. Julie and one of the men were laughing and whispering until Jayne saw a stern glance come their way from the far end of the pew.

Jayne wiggled slightly, edging herself forward. She had still not seen Bessie, the sweet old lady who had welcomed her so warmly before. Scanning the crowd, she was surprised to see Kristin sitting at the front of the church in the choir loft, a guitar beside her.

Curiosity filled Jayne, who began to wonder what Kristin was doing up there. The young girl looked radiant, she thought. In the past few weeks Kristin had blossomed under Jayne's tutelage. Not a great deal thinner, what had bloomed in Kristin was a lovely self-confidence. Once she mastered the class exercises, she had changed, now knowing that she was able to be a leader, not forever doomed to follow. Jayne had left the class with her on two separate occasions while she took phone calls and discovered she could not have given the young Kristin a more cherished gift.

Still wondering where Bessie was as the service started, Jayne discovered, at least, what

Kristin was up to. Before the sermon, Kristin stood and, clutching the guitar, walked toward the center of the church. Pulling a high stool from behind a screen, she sat down, arranging the guitar on one raised knee. Then she began to sing in a sweet, clear voice, accompanying herself on the instrument.

Entranced, Jayne barely drew a breath until the last soft note had sounded, and Kristin had returned to her place. She was certainly not the same child who had come to Body Images, plain and lumpy, head hung low! Delighted by what she had just seen, Jayne settled back, wondering. what her next surprise would be.

It wasn't long in coming.

The pastor's reverent tones were rolling over her, showering her with a tenuous peace when Bessie Norheim's name was mentioned. The pastor was asking for special prayers for Bessie who was in University Hospital for an extended stay.

Chad didn't tell me! Jayne was alarmed about the little woman's well-being. The rest of the service was lost on Jayne, who mulled over Bessie's absence from church and Chad's uncharacteristic silence on the subject. She sat rigid for the remainder of the hour, tapping her long lacquered nails against the gold clasp on her purse.

Eager now to leave, Jayne waited impatiently for the last of the congregation to file from the building, and the organist to finish the booming postlude before she slipped from her seat and out into the heat of the day.

165

Chad and Julie had left by separate doors, Jayne had observed, with nothing more than a friendly wave between them. One of Julie's brothers, however, had caught up with Chad just before he slipped out and clapped him on the back in friendly camaraderie.

Kristin was still on Jayne's mind as she made her way from her perch in the balcony, back to HighTower Court. She had watched the beaming girl receiving congratulatory hugs as the people filed from the pews. Jayne could see how tall and proud she was standing and wondered why she couldn't accomplish the same for herself.

Feeling desperately lonely, Jayne followed another impulse. Rather than taking the elevator to her apartment, she went through the building to the garage. Tapping down the stairs into the gray concrete enclosure, she headed for the sleek silver vehicle and slipped inside. The smell of new leather and fabric dye still lingered in its recesses. She longed for another fragrance— Chad's tangy, clean scent, tantalizing yet comforting.

Wind whipping through her hair, Jayne made the turns toward University Hospital. She felt the need to talk with Bessie, the one person other than Chad who had accepted her so unconditionally.

The medicinal vapors assailed her senses as she walked through the double glass doors of the hospital. The sounds and smells at Body Images were so much more healthy, so vibrant, that Jayne was again thankful she'd given up her job to join Buddy in his venture. No whispered conversations or hushed tones there, just noisy, sweaty, healthy players, invigorated and laughing. Body Images promoted wise living, wholesome fun. Jayne felt a sinking sensation in the pit of her stomach as a terrifying thought came to her. *If only I haven't jeopardized my career as well as my personal happiness!* It would break her heart to have the Body Images partnership split . . . because of her selfishness.

Still familiar with the long hospital corridors, Jayne found Bessie's room with ease. Peeking around the corner of her door, Jayne was stunned to see the little woman, lost in the expanse of a hospital bed. Her white hair faded into the whiteness of the sheets, and her skin echoed the ivory of the standard hospital gown. The only bright spots in the entire bed were Bessie's eyes, bright blue and piercing, twinkling in delight at the sight of her visitor.

"Jayne! How lovely that you came!" She held out her arms, no larger than broom handles, to embrace her, and Jayne ran into the love, gobbling it up rapaciously, with an insatiable hunger. Hugging Bessie in return, Jayne felt like she was cuddling a child, tiny and frail.

"You've lost too much weight, Bessie Norheim! Aren't they feeding you here? As a former dietitian, I still have some connections at this hospital!" Jayne scolded playfully, tears glistening on her cheeks.

"The food is pretty bad, my dear. No salt, no fat, no sugar, no taste."

The distressed look that clouded Bessie's face

167

made Jayne want to rush right out and fix her something.

"Bessie!" she exclaimed as the idea took hold. "What you need is a protein drink that Chad mixes for us at Body Images. It's gray and disgusting-looking, but it tastes wonderful. I suspect it has prunes and pecans and a lot of stranger things yet in it. But it's exactly what you need right now."

"Shall we call Chad and ask him to bring one? We could tell him it's doctor's orders. I really shouldn't have to starve to death over a broken hip."

"Why don't you wait until I leave, Bessie, and then call him. I'd rather not run into Chad right now. . . ."

"Are you two lovely young people having trouble? I can't imagine it! I know how Chad feels about you!"

"How he feels about me? If he feels anything more than disgust and disappointment, I'd be very surprised, Bessie." She paced the tiny room, bumping into the wall heater on one side and the bedside table on the other.

"Why would he be disappointed in you, dear? I don't understand." Bessie watched the agitated journey, alarmed and confused.

The whole, ugly story came pouring out then, words falling so fast Jayne stumbled over them in the telling. Bessie listened quietly, nonjudgmentally, not speaking until Jayne's outburst was stilled. Jayne laid it all before her friend—her former obesity, Ed, her plans for retribution, Chad.

"Does Chad understand this, Jayne? Does he know why you have been spending so much time with Ed these past weeks?"

"No, not really. I believe he thinks Ed is my first choice, and Chad is not the kind to interfere. A gentleman to the last, he's just faded into the background, opening the way for Ed and me. And then I didn't dare reveal that perverse plan of mine, of course. Chad is so honorable, Bessie, he would never stand for it!"

"But he's also forgiving, my dear. You've forgotten about that." Bessie smiled gently, not so shocked by the tale as Jayne had expected.

"That's been coming up a lot lately. Forgiving. Not seven times, but seventy times seven." Jayne recited the words like a pledge.

"That's right, Matthew 18, verses 21 and 22— Jesus' command to keep on forgiving."

Surprise was evident in Jayne's eyes. She had never known anyone who could actually remember and quote Bible passages like that. Bessie must have spent a lot of time studying and committing those passages to memory. But she still didn't know the whole story.

"Bessie, I really have driven Chad away. He has a new interest now. It's Julie Swenson. She goes to your church. Chad has been teaching Julie to play racquetball and handball, and they get along beautifully together. I won't interfere, Bessie. I've done too much harm to too many people as it is."

"I can't believe that Chad prefers Julie over you, Jayne. That doesn't make sense, for a lot of reasons. But I can't say until I talk to Chad."

Bessie's already wrinkled brow furrowed even deeper in thought.

"Don't mention this to Chad, please, Bessie. I have to face him myself. I want to tell him the truth. He deserves that much. But I don't think he'll ever forgive me."

"He'll forgive you, dear, and God will, too—just ask Him."

"Ask Him? What do you mean? Ask Him to forgive me for being a conniving, deceitful, vengeful person? How could He? That's quite a favor to ask, Bessie!"

"Yes it is, dear. But, you see, He's *already* forgiven you. His love and mercy are gifts. All we have to do is accept them."

"Really, Bessie? Really?"

"God doesn't lie, Jayne. He can't. Ask Him for forgiveness and believe it. You can have the same peace and reassurance that Chad and I have."

An hour later Jayne left the hospital buoyant and free, happier than she could ever remember feeling. Bessie had shown her the way to find that elusive peace she had been searching for. Now she knew what she had to do. First she must confront Ed. She had deceived him for too long. Apologies would not be enough to compensate for the pain, but they were all she could offer. Even the specter of facing Ed with the awful truth could not entirely dampen her spirits. Not now.

CHAPTER FOURTEEN

STRIDING BACK AND FORTH like a lion in an invisible cage, Ed Garrett was pacing the sidewalk in front of her apartment building when Jayne arrived. Tanned and sleek, he looked very much like the eighteen-year-old she had loved. Worry melted into anger at the sight of her. His first words were sharp with emotion.

"Where have you been? I looked for you at Body Images and then here. I even had the apartment manager check your apartment to see if you were in there, sick. The security in this place rivals Fort Knox!" Then Ed revealed exactly how worried he had been. In a low, almost inaudible, voice he said, "I finally called Chad to see if you were there—but I only succeeded in upsetting him, too. Where were you last night?"

"You must have just missed me, Ed. I fell asleep in Buddy's office on that rickety old cot of his. When I woke up, it was late, and most everyone but the janitors had gone home. So I did, too. I went for a walk early this morning and then to see a sick friend at University Hospital. I'm sorry I alarmed you so . . . I didn't realize anyone would miss me.''

"Miss you! I was worried sick! You leave your office for a few minutes and don't show up again until the next day! I waited and waited, but you never came back. It took me a long time to get up the nerve to call Chad, Jayne. I thought you were together.'' Ed's voice lowered to a whisper and there was none of the pompous arrogance left. He had been frightened and he showed it.

"Oh, Ed, I'm so terribly sorry!" Jayne laid a hand on his arm, wanting for the first time to hug him close to her. The sensitive, frightened Ed was far more appealing than the blustering bully.

"We need to talk. Come up to my apartment.'' Leading the way past the rows of silver mail-boxes and intercom security system, she opened the oversized wooden door with a turn of her key. Leading the uncharacteristically docile Ed into the elevator, Jayne punched her floor button and stood quietly, gathering her thoughts and for the second time that day, praying.

Once in the apartment, she ushered him onto the ivory sectional and offered him coffee. He had a right to be as comfortable as possible when she told him.

Ed would have none of the delaying tactics. "What's it all about, Jayne? You can quit fussing around like an old mother hen now. I know something's up.''

How could he help suspecting something? She realized too late. Love is not something you can pretend. Surely he had sensed it, too.

Drawing a deep purifying breath, she plunged in and poured out the entire sordid story, from the night he had arrived in Minneapolis.

"I've deceived you, Ed, from the first night in this apartment." Seeing the stunned, blank look on his face, she struggled for the words to express her feelings, explain her actions.

"Ed, I have loved you. When we were eighteen, I loved you more than I thought I could ever love anyone again. You were my lifeline, the first man who had ever even noticed I existed. I had feelings, emotions, dreams, just like every other girl, but my size worked against me. No one knew how much I hurt inside that body I hated. Then, you came along. You were nice to me. I realize now that that's *all* it was. You were my first date in eighteen years, Ed. I know now that a lot of what I thought was love was actually infatuation and gratitude—gratitude for helping me prove that someone as handsome and popular as you could be interested in a girl like me."

She held up a trembling hand as Ed tried to interrupt, refusing to be stopped once the floodgates had been opened.

"What a feather in my cap! Ed Garrett! Half the girls in school wanted to date you, and you asked *me* out!" She emphasized her amazement with a jabbing finger pointed at her chest. "I don't know what prompted you, but it was like finding a pot of gold at the end of a rainbow for me. It didn't last, though, Ed. You left. And you

173

probably don't even remember what you said when you did. But it's etched on my memory like a carving in granite." She paused, almost overwhelmed even ten years later. "You said, 'You're a nice girl, Jayne, but there's just too much of you.'"

Tears stained Jayne's face then, spilling through the mascara she had so studiously applied that morning.

"I've never forgotten that, Ed, and until today, I've never forgiven you, either."

"Jayne, I never knew ... I never realized...." Genuine anguish rang out in Ed's voice. He sat forward, struggling against the quicksand tugging of the couch pillows, fighting his way toward her, but she stopped him with the palm of an outstretched hand.

"There's more. Hear me out. I need to say this, Ed, and it shames me so to tell it that you mustn't interrupt. I feel so small, so petty . . . ."

Jayne paced around the room, staring at the paintings gracing the walls, unseeing. She ran her slender fingers through her hair, pulling at it from temple to crown, tugging so hard that the skin around her eyes slanted upward with the pressure. Pivoting sharply to face him, she continued.

"I was delighted to get your note, Ed, to find that you were in town. I had some things to prove. I spent ten years of my life thinking of ways to make you sorry you left me. And about a year ago, I found one. If I were slim, beautiful and successful, you'd have to realize what a mistake you made. Well, here it is—this is what you missed."

Flinging her arms wide she whirled around like a ramp model, breathtakingly beautiful.

"I've spent months—hard, hungry months—on this body, Ed. And I could tell from the moment you walked into my apartment that you liked it. Now I had my tool for revenge. I never meant to fall in love with you again, Ed. I never even meant to begin *liking* you. I just wanted you to fall for me. Once you did, I could show you how it felt to be jilted, abandoned by someone you loved."

Jayne sat down beside the man on the couch, leaning forward till their faces were close, her expression exuding the urgency she felt to make him understand.

"You were set up, Ed. Set up for a fall. But the funny part is that now I don't want you to fall. I don't want to hurt you anymore." She turned away, unwilling to see the pitiful play of emotions on his face. "I still don't love you, Ed, but I *like* you. You've changed since you came to Body Images. It has that effect on people, I think. It's a healthy, wholesome atmosphere where everyone is bent on improvement and positive change. You begin to like yourself better and that makes you like others more, too. I found that out, but it still wasn't enough. I still wanted to hurt you."

Rising, Jayne began drifting around the room again, talking as much for her own benefit as for Ed's.

"This should be the best moment of my life.

I've dreamed of it for a long time, and instead it's turning out to be distasteful and horrid. I've hurt a man I've become fond of and completely driven away the one I love . . . ."

Swiveling to face him, Jayne pleaded, "Forgive me, Ed. Forgive me for the shabby way I've treated you. You didn't deserve it; no one does. I've learned a lot about forgiving in the past twenty-four hours, and I'm in desperate need of some for myself."

Stunned and silent, Ed drooped into the ivory sectional, his hands lying limp at his sides. Jayne could see him mentally processing this startling information. A range of emotions played across his features—surprise, anger, fury and then, much to Jayne's surprise, a slight, tender smile.

After a long silence, Ed spoke. "Yes, Jayne, I forgive you. You see, I wasn't any more confident than you—I just never let it show. I've been a blustering tough guy all my life just to cover up the coward inside! Coming to Body Images and knowing you and Buddy and Chad has been a wonderful experience for me," he admitted ruefully. "Somehow I never really thought you could love me again. I've carried a lot of guilt about those days. And there's no way I could compete with Chad."

"I've driven Chad out of the picture too, Ed. He's found someone new. My little scheme really backfired, didn't it?"

"Not entirely. You opened my eyes. Those first days at Body Images, especially the ones in your exercise classes, I was so embarrassed, I think I did begin to realize how you must have

176

felt when you were heavy. You'd fold yourself into a pretzel, and I'd still be trying to touch the floor! I didn't know human beings could bend and stretch like you can. Anyway, I've trimmed a few pounds and am looking pretty good, if I do say so myself." He grinned, patting the now sleek stomach.

"You look wonderful, Ed. Handsome as when I first met you!" Jayne's face softened into a smile. Ed was being unbelievably understanding. Forgiving . . . seventy times seven.

"That good, huh?" He laughed and Jayne had to join in, grabbing his extended hands.

"I love you, Jayne, but enough to know that I have to leave. I know you love Chad. I've known it all along, but I guess I had to try. In all fairness, Chad allowed me every opportunity to win you back, but I still couldn't do it. I won't hurt you again by staying around, pulling you apart. My business is nearly wrapped up here and my weekly membership is due at Body Images if I stick around, so I think this is the time to call it quits. Friends?"

"Oh, Ed! Friends—always friends!" Jayne ran into his warm embrace, savoring the peaceful feeling spilling over her. Her ten-year ordeal was over. The ghosts that had haunted her were put to rest. They had both grown up. *Forgive* and *forget*—what wonderful words!

Still gripping her by the shoulders, Ed held her at arm's length in front of him. "Friends can tell each other things, can't they?"

"Anything, Ed, anything!" She beamed at

him, for the first time really showing him the dazzling quality of her beauty.

"As much as I wanted to hate Chad, I couldn't. I knew where my competition was and I had a hard time generating enough energy to try to stop it. Don't let him get away. If he turned to Julie, it was only because he was too much of a gentleman to horn in on me." Ed's face took on a dark intensity as he spoke. "Chad's talked to me about his faith and has given me some pretty powerful things to think about. I don't feel I've come out of this a loser, Jayne. I just didn't win the things I expected to. I think we've grown up. Let's lay the past to rest."

Seeing Ed leave was far more painful than Jayne had imagined it could be. Walking him to his car across the plush green lawn, Jayne's steps lagged as time for the final good-by approached.

"Will you be in tomorrow to pick up your gear at Body Images?" Putting it off for a day might help.

"No. You know me—have duffel bag, will travel. I've already packed the car. Buddy told me I couldn't have a locker unless I paid for a full four months!"

"That stinker! He's been difficult for you from the start, hasn't he?"

"He's been protecting you, Jayne. Buddy saw trouble coming long before you did. And actually, we've gotten to be friends, in a roundabout sort of way. It all started while you were in San Francisco. He decided to give me a break. He's coming up to Canada to hunt with me this fall. I know the best goose hunting locations, and I figure, if I'm going to be safe in the wilderness, he's the best possible hunting companion. No wild animal would dare attack that mountain-sized man!"

"You two! And I thought you hated each other!" Punching him playfully in the arm, Jayne scolded. "I spent all that time playing peacemaker and you didn't need it at all!"

"Oh, we did at first. He couldn't stand the sight of me. Don't blame him, actually. I was a real pain in the neck. Well, Jayne, here's the car. Guess this is good-by."

Throwing her arms around his neck, Jayne hugged Ed with an intensity born of fondness and frustration. Cheeks pressed tightly together, she could feel his heart beating steadily in his chest. Finally releasing her stranglehold, she looked into his eyes, touched his cheek with one oval nail, lifted a trembling finger to her lips, kissed it softly and returned it to his cheek.

"By, Ed. Thanks."

She stood on the sidewalk, watching until the car disappeared from sight around a sprawling building and then stared a while longer at the point at which it had vanished. Now there was but one loose end to tie up. And it would hurt even more than this one.

CHAPTER FIFTEEN

EMOTIONALLY EXHAUSTED, Jayne delayed her visit to Chad, hoping that a warm bath and a few hours' sleep would revive her enough to get her through the ordeal. She had hedged as long as she could. But after the previous sleepless night, her energy was at a low ebb.

Schlumping around in her oldest robe, a chenille affair that made her feel very much like an unmade bed, she puttered with her plants and read the Sunday paper, knowing consciously that she was in the eye of the storm.

She felt so unlike herself that she had not even combed her hair. Dark waves curled at random around her shoulders and tumbled forward as she stooped to pick up a stray section of the paper lying on the floor. Her eyes caught the small red New Testament lying on the coffee table, and she picked it up on her way by, tossing both it and the sports section onto the pile of papers.

Plopping down on the sectional, she put her slippered feet onto the coffee table, mindless of the costly artwork exhibited there, and picked up the little Testament.

Bessie had insisted she take it. "I have several others, dear. You take this one. You'll want to read it."

She had accepted reluctantly. Bessie had already given her so much. Opening it to First Corinthians, she started to read. Her eyes fell on the last two verses of the sixth chapter.

> Do you not know that your body is a temple of the Holy Spirit within you, which you have from God? You are not your own, you were bought with a price. So glorify God in your body.

It was as though a blinding light flickered on in her brain. *Finally* she understood Chad's motivation for helping Buddy develop Body Images. Just as in everything else in Chad's life, he wanted to do God's will.

And another thought crept into Jayne's consciousness. Here was the *real* reason for caring for one's body. Ed and her scheme for revenge had vanished, but an even stronger purpose remained. She, too, could help others fulfill this simple command to glorify God—and Body Images was her tool.

Just then the doorbell rang. Jayne cast an irritating glance in its direction, wanting to ignore it. Finally curiosity won out and she got up to answer, flipping on the visual screen.

In full view was Chad, tapping his foot in that unconscious and so familiar way. But he was different somehow—older, more thoughtful, tired-looking. His brow was creased with a frown and he appeared worried by the lack of response from within the apartment.

"Hi, Chad." She greeted him through the intercom and some of the concern faded from his face.

"Jayne! Can I come up? I've been terribly worried about you!"

"I'm okay. Come on up." There was to be no rest before she faced him. Perhaps it was best to get it over with, anyway.

Before she could open the door, he was there pounding.

"How you can beat me to my own door is beyond me, Chad." She greeted him pleasantly. He was a wonderful sight. She would savor each moment with him, to remember when he left her.

"Exercise. Lots of it. And long legs. Where have you been?" He catapulted into the room, then came to a sudden halt, surprised by the uncharacteristic clutter of papers and pillows.

"I'm sorry if I alarmed anyone. I fell asleep on Buddy's cot last night and didn't get back to the apartment until late. Then I went to visit your friend Bessie at University Hospital today, and I've been home since."

"I just came from seeing Bessie myself. I've been worried ever since Ed called. I could tell he was alarmed by your absence. At least Bessie told me you were all right."

Jayne's stomach plummeted. Chad had seen Bessie. Just how much had she told him?

182

"Just exactly what *did* Bessie tell you, Chad?"
Perhaps she was worrying in vain.

"Everything, I think. Jayne . . ."

"Oh, Chad, I wanted to tell you about Ed myself!" Jayne wailed her dismay. Then, having begun, she blurted out the whole story, her words tumbling over one another in her haste. "I thought if I could explain, it wouldn't sound so cold and calculating. It was a hideous scheme, I know, leading him on when I didn't care for him, just to treat him the way he once treated me. I didn't know how to forgive then, Chad. I've paid for that lack of knowledge for ten years! I wanted desperately to make him pay for jilting me, but when it came time for me to turn the tables on him, all my anger was gone! I'd learned to like Ed again, and—I fell in love with *you*. Now I've lost you both. Why didn't I know about 'an eye for an eye' and 'forgiving seventy times seven' before it was too late?"

The confusion on Chad's face grew as Jayne uttered her garbled confession. Finally a smile began to play across his lips. Fear shot through Jayne then like an icy bolt, shimmering inside her.

"*That's* not what Bessie told me, Jayne! She told me about you becoming a Christian!"

"What?" Jayne's jaw dropped, and she stared at him in disbelief. Now what would he think of her?

"That's what counts, Jayne, not whatever it is you've been babbling about. Buddy spilled the beans about that. I stopped at his place on the way over here. He was worried about you, too. I

183

guess he didn't realize how long you'd been asleep in his office."

"Buddy told you everything?"

"That word *everything*—that's where we lost communication before. He told me about your plan to punish Ed. And he told me Ed's side, too."

"Ed's side?" Jayne questioned weakly. Apparently Buddy was a veritable storehouse of information once he started talking.

"Ed talked about you and how pretty you were when he first knew you. He said you were so self-conscious about your weight that you scared everyone else away. He told Buddy that he'd been pretty cruel to you, but he hadn't realized just how cruel until he came to Body Images and found himself the one with a far from perfect body." Chad grinned as he straightened the saggy shoulders on Jayne's worn robe.

"Chad, do you understand all this? Do you realize what I've been saying?" Jayne marveled at Chad's calm acceptance.

"Yes and no. I don't understand why all this fuss. You're pretty on the inside and that's what counts. Looking the way you do on the outside is just a bonus."

"But you're so handsome yourself, Chad!"

"Am I?" He seemed genuinely surprised by her statement. "That's nice. But it's not the outside of a person that you learn to love. I love you and I love Bessie and there's no comparing looks there!"

"Bessie? But what about Julie?"

"What about her?" Chad was now cheerfully

roaming around the room, poking a curious finger at the weavings and pottery vases, fingering dainty collectibles, increasingly confident under Jayne's teary glare. His broad shoulders rolled casually under his black poplin jacket.

"What about her? Chad, you're in love with her!" Jayne nearly roared with frustration. He was acting so strangely. Perhaps this was his way of punishing her.

"I am?" He paused in his journey, holding a crystal globe which he began to toss from hand to hand in careless abandon. "Who says?"

"I say, Chad. It's been so apparent. You've hardly spent any time apart for the last few weeks. I've seen you—mopping her brow and hugging her. You come together in the morning, and, except for your classes, you're with Julie all day long!"

"That's what I get paid to do." The worried look in Chad's eyes was diminishing rapidly, replaced by impish glee.

"Paid? Who paid you—and to do what?" Something strange was going on here.

"Julie's fiancé paid me to teach her to play racquetball, handball and squash. He'a a pro, but with Julie, he's a complete bust as a teacher. It seems they can't keep their minds on the game in those little rooms."

"*Fiancé!* Julie's fiancé?"

"Do you realize that you're becoming very repetitive?" Chad's casual, bantering air was finally making his point. "Mike Hedrick, Julie's *fiancé*, and one of her three brothers were in my fraternity at college. We all used to play together, but neither of them could seem to teach Julie the game. They asked me to give her a crash course before the wedding. I think Mike thinks they're going to play racquetball on their honeymoon, but I think he has another thing coming!''

Stunned, Jayne slumped back on the couch and muttered, ''But Julie has four brothers. I saw them in church.''

''Correction, she has three brothers—and Mike. I talked to him after the service. And why didn't you let me know you were there?'' For the first time, irritation crept into Chad's voice. ''I could have saved you a lot of misery if you'd only felt free to tell me what was troubling you!''

''But I thought Julie . . . .'' Her words trailed away.

''Did you think I'd jump into one girl's arms when I'm in love with another? Granted, I was biding my time to see what would happen between you and Ed. I prayed for whatever was God's will. Then I waited . . . and played a lot of racquetball and lifted a lot of weights and did some running. I think now I'm finally getting the answer.''

Suddenly Jayne shot up, eyes squinting in a distrustful glare. ''Did Buddy know about this?''

''Sure he did. Being everybody's sounding board, he knows everything. He just never tells. He wouldn't have let us get too far afield, but I believe he thought we should work things out for ourselves.''

''That Buddy . . . .'' Jayne's mind was churning with what she would tell him.

''You look like you need a good meal, Jayne,

or a power-packed protein punch. How about it?" Chad was appraising the thin arms and legs sticking out of the shapeless garment.

"And *you* look like you need a haircut. I noticed it in church." Pacing behind the couch, Jayne paused to touch the feathers of his hair and was amazed by its silky softness. Impulsively burying her nose in its depths, she could smell the fresh, manly scent. "Oh, Chad, I was so afraid you would hate me!"

Chad tipped his head back and grinned up at her from the slouching position he had taken on the couch. Grabbing Jayne by the wrists, he pulled her across his shoulders and onto his lap. She curled into his chest, immediately content.

"I could never hate you. I wouldn't have approved of what you were doing, but I would still love you. We're human. We make mistakes. But if God is willing to forgive us, can we do less than forgive each other?"

"Oh, Chad." The words were a whisper in the still room.

"Jayne, will you marry me?" The guise of bravado slipping, Chad appeared as if his very existence hung on her answer.

"You mean—in spite of—everything?"

"In spite of—or maybe because of—everything."

Barely pausing to draw a breath, Jayne threw both arms around him. "Yes, Chad, a million times, yes!"

Wrapping her in his strong arms he kissed her, wiping out the past.

Some moments later, Chad bolted up, nearly tipping the glowing Jayne off his lap.

"Let's go and get a power-packed protein punch at the club. Maybe Buddy's there and we can tell him about our new merger."

"And after that, a steak maybe—fried potatoes and dessert!" Suddenly ravenous, Jayne jumped at the idea.

"But what about your diet?"

"What about it? Now the new Jayne Lindstrom is complete. For once I'm going to celebrate!"

ABOUT THE AUTHOR

JUDY BAER, an honor graduate of Concordia College, is a wife, a homemaker, and mother of two young daughters. On her birthday, her husband surprised her with a word processor, agreeing to renew the lease each year she completed a book! *Love's Perfect Image* is her second, with another Serenade Serenata scheduled for next year.

Judy writes not only for the joy of writing, but to convey her belief that Christians are granted the greatest freedom to fulfill their potential and to find joy in each other and in Him.

A Letter To Our Readers

Dear Reader:

Pioneering is an exhilarating experience, filled with opportunities for exploring new frontiers. The Zondervan Corporation is proud to be the first major publisher to launch a series of inspirational romances designed to inspire and uplift as well as to provide wholesome entertainment. In order that we might better contribute to your reading enjoyment, we would appreciate your taking a few minutes to respond to the following questions and return to:

> Anne Severance, Editor
> Serenade/Saga Books
> 749 Templeton Drive
> Nashville, Tennessee   37205

1. Did you enjoy reading LOVE'S PERFECT IMAGE?
   - ☐ Very much. I would like to see more books by this author!
   - ☐ Moderately
   - ☐ I would have enjoyed it more if _____

2. Where did you purchase this book? _____

3. What influenced your decision to purchase this book?
   - ☐ Cover
   - ☐ Title
   - ☐ Publicity
   - ☐ Back cover copy
   - ☐ Friends
   - ☐ Other _____

4. Please rate the following elements from 1 (poor) to 10 (superior):

   ☐ Heroine   ☐ Plot
   ☐ Hero   ☐ Inspirational theme
   ☐ Setting   ☐ Secondary characters

5. Which settings would you like to see in future Serenade/Saga Books?

   _____   _____

   _____   _____

6. What are some inspirational themes you would like to see treated in Serenade books?

   _____   _____

   _____   _____

7. Would you be interested in reading other Serenade/Serenata or Serenade/Saga Books?

   ☐ Very interested
   ☐ Moderately interested
   ☐ Not interested

8. Please indicate your age range:

   ☐ Under 18   ☐ 25–34   ☐ 46–55
   ☐ 18–24   ☐ 35–45   ☐ Over 55

9. Would you be interested in a Serenade book club? If so, please give us your name and address:

   Name _____

   Occupation _____

   Address _____

   City _____ State _____ Zip _____

Serenade/Serenata Books are inspirational romances in contemporary settings, designed to bring you a joyful, heart-lifting reading experience.

Other Serenade books available in your local book-store:

Coming in the months ahead:

Serenade/Saga Books are historical inspirational romances, and are available wherever Serenade Books are sold.

Date Due